& Dramas

...Plus!

IS IT NEW YEAR, NEW YOU?
TRY OUR FAB QUIZ AT
THE BACK OF THE BOOK

SOME SECRETS ARE JUST TOO GOOD TO KEEP
TO YOURSELF!

Sugar Secrets...

Sugar
SECRETS...

...& Dramas

Mel Sparke

Collins

An Imprint of HarperCollinsPublishers

Published in Great Britain by Collins in 1999
Collins is an imprint of HarperCollins*Publishers*Ltd
77–85 Fulham Palace Road, Hammersmith, London W6 8JB

The HarperCollins website address is
www.**fire**and**water**.com

9 8 7 6 5 4 3 2 1

Creative consultant: Sue Dando
Copyright © Sugar 1999. Licensed with TLC

ISBN 0 00 675429 5

Printed and bound in Great Britain by
Caledonian International Book Manufacturing Ltd, Glasgow

CHAPTER 1

● ●

MAKING PLANS

"What about a nice big pair of scissors?"

"What kind of present idea is that, Matt?" asked Sonja.

"It's the perfect gift for Ollie – it means he could finally lose that Shaggy from *Scooby Doo* haircut of his."

"Oi – there's nothing wrong with my hair!" protested Ollie Stanton.

Kerry Bellamy reached up and stroked the straight, light-brown locks that flopped endearingly over her boyfriend's handsome face.

No, there's definitely nothing wrong with his hair – or anything else, she thought to herself.

"Or a new pair of trainers," said Catrina Osgood, wrinkling her nose and pointing to Ollie's battered footwear. "Those are *well* past their sell-by date."

"But these are my favourites!"

"*I* know!" grinned Sonja, ignoring Ollie's whingeing. "How about a life-sized, framed picture of Kerry that you can keep beside your bed and kiss last thing at night?"

"Yeah!" Cat joined in, clapping her hands together. "Maya can take one of those corny, soft-focus photos like you see advertised in the back of magazines!"

"No, Maya could *not*," growled Maya from the comfort of the biggest bean bag in Matt's den.

Kerry fingered her infuriatingly unruly curls, thought of her sprinkling of freckles and laughed at the idea of being transformed by trick photography.

"OK, so I appreciate your help," she smiled at her mates, who were sprawled lazily at various points around the large basement room. "But I think I can sort out Ollie's Christmas present myself. As for the photo, it's not like I can really see myself as this doe-eyed, romantic figure, clutching a flower and done out all sepia-toned..."

As Kerry jokingly struck a pose, her friends all had the same thought at once: with her chin tilted up and her red-brown hair tumbling down her back, she looked *exactly* like a doe-eyed, romantic figure.

But that was the trouble – where everyone else saw a pretty girl, Kerry was convinced she was nothing next to the blonde, honey-toned beauty of her best friend Sonja Harvey. Or nowhere near the loveliness of Maya Joshi, whose Indian background gave her almond eyes to die for and dark hair so glossy that she could have advertised conditioners on the telly.

"Well, I don't know about that, Kerry," Anna Michaels smiled from the comfort of the big sofa she was sharing with Joe Gladwin. "I think you'd look great. But *I* think it would be better if Santa brought Ollie a new alarm clock, considering the number of times he's been late for his shift at the café recently."

Ollie clasped his hands to his chest and groaned as if Anna's pointed words had hit their target.

"Ouch! That's not fair, Anna – you know it's because my Vespa's packed up a couple of times on the way to work."

Now it was time for all the others to groan.

"Ollie, get rid of that stupid bike! It never works!" Matt Ryan teased him.

"It does!" replied Ollie indignantly. "It's working now..."

"Yeah, but for how long?" laughed Sonja.

"Anyway," said Ollie, changing the subject,

"I've told Kerry she doesn't need to get me anything for Christmas. I've already got the best present in the world... which is her."

"Bleurrrgh!" Cat's face contorted and she pretended to stick her fingers down her throat, while everyone else winced and pulled disgusted faces.

"What?!" Ollie objected, blinking in mock innocence. "What have I said?"

"That is *sooo* soppy!" Cat complained. "I can't believe you said it in front of everyone, Ol."

"But it's true," grinned Ollie, knowing he'd wound his friends up.

Kerry squirmed a little as he wrapped his arms around her; she was half delighted by what he'd just said and half flustered by such a public declaration.

"That may well be, but do you have to *tell* everyone?" Sonja let out an exaggerated sigh and winked at Kerry to let her know she was only teasing.

"Hey, guys, lay off him," scolded Matt. "You wouldn't be barfing if a girl had said that – you'd be all gooey-eyed and cooing about how wonderful it was. Anyway, I go along with what Ollie's saying for me and Gaby too – I'm just happy to have her. You lot are just jealous because *you're* not in love."

Gabrielle Adjani – who'd just padded down

the stairs – caught the tail-end of the conversation. She let out a little squeal of embarrassment, then ran over and playfully punched Matt as she fell on to the bean bag beside him.

"Crikey, *you've* changed," Cat snickered at Matt. "A few months ago you'd have been the first one to scoff at any kind of smoochiness. Now look at you. A perfect picture of loved-upness. No offence to Gabrielle, but frankly, I'm waiting for the bubble to burst."

Cat immediately slapped her hand over her mouth, her eyes bulging with the shock of what she'd just said. She wasn't exactly known for her subtlety, but even *she* realised she was being tactless. It was the sort of thing she could usually get away with saying in front of Matt, but not when Gabrielle was there too. The horrified looks on everyone's faces confirmed this.

"I'm really sorry, Gaby," Cat squirmed. "That just kind of slipped out. I didn't mean it to sound so harsh. The truth is, I've never seen Matt look happier. I was just being my usual bitchy self."

"That's OK, Cat," Gabrielle answered generously. "Now that I finally know all about Matt's stream of exes..." She turned and began her pretend punching again.

"...I guess I can understand why you might think that way."

Matt gave his girlfriend a wobbly smile and almost looked like he actually deserved the thumping she was giving him. Although when he'd first met her, Matt had tried to reinvent himself as someone with a clean record when it came to relationships, Gabrielle was now well up to speed on his lurid past.

At first, he'd just confessed to two ex-girlfriends – Cat, and Ollie's twin sister – but soon after, he'd told her the whole truth. There were just too many girls in Winstead and the surrounding area who could land him in it at any time and Gabrielle deserved to hear the truth from him. Luckily, she'd taken it pretty well.

"At least Winstead will be a safer place this year without Matt trying to charm Christmas kisses out of every girl that gets in his line of vision!" Sonja teased him, feeling it was safe to do so if Gabrielle didn't have a problem with it. "What were you *like* at that Christmas Eve party we went to?"

"You may mock," he shot back, "but you're no angel yourself, Ms Harvey. Didn't you and Cat have a snogging contest at that party? Weren't the two of you running around with plastic mistletoe all night, seeing who could get the most kisses?"

"Hey, the only reason we started that was because *you* inspired us with your sterling snogging efforts," Cat pointed out with a wicked smile on her face. "What was your score again – wasn't it twelve different girls, beating your previous best of nine the year before?"

Matt shuffled till his bean bag rustled. He knew when he was beaten.

· "Are you thinking of having a party here this year, Matt?" Joe butted in, keen to get the conversation back on an even keel. Once Cat got going, she could end up saying almost anything, and it usually got worse rather than better. She always found it hard to find the fine line between taking the mick and going too far.

"God, no. Why would he?" snorted Cat. "He doesn't need to have parties now that he's an old married man. He only ever held them in the past so he could get his lips round a bit of totty."

"Actually, yes, Joe. I probably will have a bit of a bash, and you'll all be invited," Matt said, before adding pointedly, "Except Cat, that is."

"I doubt I would have been able to fit you in anyway," Cat replied with a haughty tilt of her head. "What with one thing and another, my diary is virtually full from now until New Year."

"What about you, Ol?" Joe asked. "Same old madness for you this Christmas?"

"Too right. I know it's not for another three weeks, but the pub's getting busy already. I'll be lucky if I get the chance to go to any parties, I'll be too busy helping my parents out when I'm not working at the End." Ollie worked for his uncle at the End-of-the-Line café and lived with his parents above The Swan pub.

"Sounds ideal," said Cat. "A party every night in your own house. No cabs to book, no worries about getting home, you just fall into bed upstairs ready for the next one tomorrow."

"Don't you believe it," said Ollie. "The whole thing is one big rush from start to finish. Christmas is supposed to be about families getting together and being nice, and we're so stressed out we're at each other's throats by the end of it."

"Poo-ey! Me and Mum are like that all year round," Cat said. "If anything, we're worse at Christmas because we have to spend so much time together. That's the worst thing about it – being forced to be nice to your family just because it's Christmas. And failing. Miserably."

"Cheers, Cat," said Sonja and gave her cousin a withering look. "That's you crossed off my present list."

"I didn't mean *your* side of the family – I'm talking about my God-awful mother," Cat drawled. "And don't pretend that you and your folks are looking forward to seeing her sour face at

Christmas dinner round yours! It's at times like this that I envy people like you, Anna. At least you've got your own place to escape to when you get sick of playing happy families."

Cat's words struck a chord with Maya.

"What about you, Anna?" she said, concerned. "What are you up to for Christmas?"

Anna felt flustered as the focus of attention fell on her. So far she had hung back from the conversation. In fact, until now, she had managed to block out all thoughts of Christmas. She was dreading the whole event; it held so many bad memories for her.

This time last year she had spent Christmas at her friend Lucy's in Exeter, and while the family had made her feel welcome, Anna felt she was intruding the whole time she was there. And the year before... well, there hadn't been much to be glad about back then.

She stumbled over her words when she answered. "I... er, I d-don't know, yet. I really haven't decided. Christmas isn't the best time for me, what with one thing and another."

Determined not to divulge any more and desperate to move the conversation on, she added quickly, "What about you, Maya – your family's Hindu, isn't it? What do you do at Christmas?"

Maya realised that Anna didn't want to talk, so she let the subject drop. "Actually, my family's a bit of a muddle when it comes to religion; my dad's Hindu, and Mum's side's Muslim and Christian. But neither of my parents are particularly religious. We just tend to have my Grandpa Naseem and my Nana Jean to visit and make it special that way."

"Sounds complicated," said Anna.

"It is," agreed Maya, aware that Anna didn't know about her parents' unconventional marriage and the trouble it had caused.

"How long is Nick shutting the End for, Ol?" Joe asked. "He hasn't asked me about doing any shifts yet once term ends, and I thought he might have done by now."

"He reckons the caff and the record shop will be open until Christmas Eve, then they'll both be closed until New Year's Day," replied Ollie.

"So you'll get a week off?" Cat said. "That's not so bad. I thought Nick would be too mean to shut for that long!"

"Well, it wouldn't surprise me," joked Ollie. "I can still see him changing his mind and deciding to open from Boxing Day onwards. Then me and Anna will be *really* hacked off."

If only you knew how wrong you were, Ol, Anna thought ruefully.

The truth was, she wished the café *could* stay open all over Christmas. At least then she wouldn't have time to get depressed about spending it on her own.

CHAPTER 2

● ●

OH NO HE'S NOT

Anna picked up the phone and punched in the number she knew off by heart.

The conversation she'd had about Christmas with the rest of the gang on Saturday night had been rattling around in her head ever since and she knew she had to do something about it.

Mooching around on Christmas Day all alone in her tiny flat above the End-of-the-Line café just seemed too sad. She knew it was a long shot, but she was keeping her fingers crossed that Owen could come and keep her company...

Absent-mindedly, Anna brushed a bit of dust off the top of the phone while she listened to the number register then begin to ring at the other end. Her face lit up when she heard her brother pick up.

"Owen? Hi, it's me. How are you?"

"Hi, Anna! I'm great, how about you?"

She felt the warm smile in her brother's voice and immediately felt happier.

"Yeah, I'm fine – up to my elbows in chip fat as usual," she joked. "Look, I know we only spoke a few days ago, but I've been thinking about Christmas..."

"Actually, me too. What have you got planned?"

"Well, that's just it," Anna said. "Nothing. Which is why I'm phoning."

"I don't suppose you'd consider coming home for Christmas?" Owen asked.

She'd expected, but not hoped for, this particular suggestion. "I couldn't, Owen. Not yet. I wouldn't feel comfortable."

"Oh, Anna, please think about it," he pleaded in a gentle tone. "Mum would love it if we were both there; it would make her year. Please don't dismiss it just like that."

"So does that mean you're definitely going to Mum's?" asked Anna, disappointment in her voice.

"Yeah, like always. I know it's been years since Dad died, but I couldn't just leave her on her own at this time of year."

Anna immediately felt guilty, even after all the

pain her mother had caused her when she'd needed her most. But guilt wasn't enough to drive her home.

"Look, why don't you think about it and let me or Mum know nearer the time?" Owen's voice was pleading now. He really did want this year to be a Michaels' family reunion.

"I'm not sure, Owen," Anna replied. "I know Mum and I are speaking again these days, but it's not like we're the best of pals all of a sudden. When we ring each other up the conversation's still pretty stilted. I really don't think I can bring myself to spend Christmas playing happy families; not after all that's happened."

"I figured you might say that," said Owen. "I understand how you must feel, but I thought that with it being Christmas and everything... God, I sound like a proper Good Samaritan, don't I?" he laughed down the line. "It's OK, Anna, you can tell me to keep my nose out of it if you like..."

"It's all right," Anna replied. "I don't mind. I'll think about it, OK?"

"Sure. So what have you been up to since we last spoke – did you go to Matt's on Saturday night?"

"Yeah, it was fun."

"All the gang there?"

"Uh-huh."

"Sonja there?"

Anna grinned. She'd wondered how long it would be before Owen brought the subject round to Sonja.

"Yes, Owen, Sonja was there. On her own and no doubt pining for you all evening."

"Don't take the mick, I was only asking," Owen said cheerfully. "I just wanted to know if she's, well, OK and everything."

"What are you asking me for? You two speak to each other on the phone more than me and you do!" teased Anna. Then a thought struck her. "Actually, Owen, couldn't you tell Mum you're not going home just this once, because you're coming to see Sonja instead? Mum could always go to Aunt Theresa's or somebody's. And that way, I'd get to spend some time with you and you'd get to see the love of your life."

Owen said nothing for a moment.

He must be tempted! Anna hoped silently.

"Anna, I love you, but I care about Mum too – and I owe it to her to be around at Christmas," he sighed. "Sonja will be busy with her own family stuff anyway."

"OK," said Anna in a small voice. She felt well and truly chastised by her big brother, even if he hadn't meant it that way.

"Anyway, what will you do if you don't come

to Mum's? You won't stay in that flat all on your own, will you?"

"Oh, no," Anna replied a little too quickly. "Don't worry about me; there'll be plenty going on around here on Christmas Day."

Only none of it will involve me, she thought, as a wave of loneliness hit her.

• • •

Cat walked into the classroom at the college which was doubling up as the combined make-up and costume area for the Drama Department's Christmas production of Cinderella, and began setting out her overloaded box of cosmetics. As usual, she was the first one there.

As chief make-up artist for the cast, over the last few weeks she'd been practising on various members, including Cinderella and the Ugly Sisters. Not having had too much experience of theatrical make-up so far on her beauty therapy course, Cat was keen to do a good job and was happy putting in the extra hours after college if it meant she'd get the actors' individual looks perfect on the night.

Apart from that, being around actors was what Cat wanted to experience: according to her skewed logic, getting into telly and film work through being a make-up artist was a short-cut to getting into acting. Make contacts, get known – and all without the bother of having to study stuff like Shakespeare and Chekhov for years. Or so Cat reckoned.

For someone who was desperate to act, being involved back stage with the pantomime was also a chance for Cat to soak up the atmosphere. She usually hung around after her stint was over, listening to the cast read through their lines, wishing *she* was Cinderella and not Fran Stevens, who in Cat's opinion had to be the most inappropriate Cinders she'd ever laid eyes on.

(*Since when was Cinderella a six-footer?* Cat thought cruelly as she eyed up the gangly Fran one day. *She's going to have to bend her knees under her frock or she'll tower over Prince Charming...*)

Cat swung round as she heard the door open. She was expecting it to be Fran, so was surprised when she saw that it was Jeff Patterson, the college's Head of English and Drama, and director of the panto. He had a pile of scripts under one arm, his mobile phone and overstuffed briefcase in the other, and a stressed look on his face.

"Hi, Jeff," Cat smiled. "You're early. I didn't expect you for another half an hour."

He gave her a tense smile in return.

"Got a lot on my mind, Catrina," he said gruffly. "I needed to get here early to try and sort this damn mess out."

Hauling his briefcase on to a table top, he dumped the huge wodge of scripts down beside it and began rifling through the case.

"Anything I can help with?" offered Cat. "I'm working on Fran today, but she hasn't turned up yet so I'm all yours."

"You'll have a long wait," he sighed, running his hand agitatedly through his shock of grey-flecked hair. "She's the reason we're in a mess. She phoned earlier; she's got glandular fever. She's out of the show."

"You're kidding!" Cat gasped, although she knew from his face that he most definitely was not joking. "Well, that's tough luck for Fran, but what's the problem? Abigail Whatsername can take over. She's her understudy..."

"*Was* her understudy. She chucked the course in a couple of days ago and went back home to Scotland. And call me reckless," he added with an ironic smile, "but I didn't think there was the need to have an *under*-understudy."

"So what will you do?" asked Cat, a glint creeping into her eyes.

"Haven't a clue. Getting someone else to learn

her lines and songs in this short a time is going to take a miracle."

Cat gazed at the lecturer as he took off his thick-rimmed glasses and began rubbing his eyes with one hand. She'd come to know him reasonably well over the last few weeks. He was approachable, practical and – at this moment – desperate.

Do it, she told herself sternly.

Without any warning, Cat threw her arms out and began belting out a song from the show at the top of her voice.

Two minutes later, Jeff was still blinking at her in astonishment through spec-free eyes.

"What was that?" he asked, once his slack-jawed mouth had moved back into action.

"*Some Day My Prince Will Come*. Don't say you didn't recognise it!" said Cat slightly huffily. Her singing voice (though only normally let loose in the shower) wasn't all *that* bad, she was sure.

"Yes, I know what the song was, Catrina," he said, still looking at her quizzically. "Maybe what I should have said was 'why?'"

"Isn't it obvious?"

"Erm, no, I'm afraid it isn't," Jeff shook his head.

"What about *me*?"

Jeff slipped his glasses back on and narrowed

his eyes, taking in the vision that was Cat: bleached blonde hair with streaks on either side of her face that matched her burgundy lipstick, a crimson, satiny T-shirt that strained alarmingly across her double D-cup chest and a black suede mini that showed an acre of thigh until her legs met her knee-high platform boots.

"What *about* you, Catrina?" the lecturer asked, raising an eyebrow.

"Let me try for the part," Cat gabbled, finding herself grabbing on to the arm of his grey wool jacket. "Go on, *pleeeeeeeease!!*"

"But Catrina – you're not even on the drama course!" protested Jeff.

"Yeah, maybe," shrugged Cat, determined not to be put off. "But I *do* know all of Cinderella's lines; I've been listening to Fran practise them for weeks. I've even helped her go through them!"

"Cat," he said gently, "while I admire your confidence, you have to understand that there's no way I could put you up there on stage in front of a couple of hundred people when you've had no acting experience before in your life. Surely you can see that?"

"Actually, no. I can't," Cat said defiantly. "What I *can* see though is a production that's going to fail – with a capital F – if you don't do something drastic. And that something is *me*."

Good speech, she praised herself, then saw from Jeff's expression that he still wasn't convinced. She had to think fast.

"Anyway, you don't know *everything* about me. I *have* had acting experience; I was involved in several plays at school."

"Really?" nodded Jeff slowly.

"Really," Cat nodded back. OK, so there hadn't been several plays – only one, and the school happened to be primary. But she had made a brilliant angel in her reception class's production of the Nativity.

Jeff looked from Cat to the pile of stapled pages that lay in front of him, then gave a sigh.

"OK, Catrina – I'll give it a shot," he said, tossing her a script. "Let's have a read-through now."

Cat tried to subdue the grin of triumph that was threatening to break out over her face.

So, I had to tell a little lie to get his attention, she thought. *But isn't acting all about making stuff up?*

CHAPTER 3

• •

DECISIONS, DECISIONS

Sonja was sitting up straight, her hands doing as much talking as her mouth.

On the red vinyl banquette opposite her, Kerry sat with her chin in her hands, her elbows slumped on the Formica table and her gaze drifting more often out of the window than towards her friend.

"The thing is, I could do a Media Studies degree, with Public Relations as a module, or I could go for a straight degree in PR. Only I can't decide which..."

Sonja started flicking once again through the university prospectuses fanned out in front of her. Kerry's own smaller pile of leaflets and information packs were still in her bag, untouched and unread.

"Well, what's the point in going for a broader-based degree if you already know that you definitely want to get into PR?" Kerry stirred herself long enough to ask. "I mean, you've been saying for the past two years that you want a job in PR, so why bother doing a course that's less specific?"

"I know," Sonja nodded, "but I keep wondering whether I'll be limiting myself in the future if I specialise so early on. I might decide half-way through the degree that I don't like PR. *Then* what?"

Kerry frowned.

"It's not like you to be so indecisive, Son," she said. "That's usually what you're telling me off for. What's up?"

"Oh, I dunno," Sonja sighed, slumping down to match Kerry's pose. "I think I've lost a bit of confidence lately."

"How d'you mean?"

"Well, I sometimes think I can't trust my own judgement any more. Like with the modelling thing – I tried so hard to convince myself it was going to be such a cool thing to get into; and even when I saw how ropy that agency was, I still nearly found myself in an advertising campaign for the local dog trimmer."

"OK, so it wasn't exactly Gucci level stuff, but

you got out of it before you ended up posing alongside any poodles!"

Both girls managed a giggle.

"Yeah, but it's also the uncertainty with Owen. I mean, I know he likes me, and I know I like him, but I don't really know what I am to him."

"What, you mean you don't know if you're proper girlfriend/boyfriend?" Kerry asked, glad to be off the subject of universities and courses.

"Exactly," nodded Sonja. "You and Ollie see loads of each other, and know exactly what your relationship is, but *we've* never said. And with Owen living so far away, and me never knowing when I'll next see him, I still can't help worrying that I'm just a nice diversion till he meets someone closer at hand."

"Who can say for sure?" Kerry smiled reassuringly at her best mate. "Maybe you'll be together for ages and maybe you won't. But take it from a girl who worries too much: stop wasting your time stressing out and just enjoy what you've got. Owen's great, you're great; you're happy when you talk to each other and see each other. That's pretty good going, isn't it?"

"Thanks, Kez, that's really sweet," Sonja beamed at her friend.

She glanced down at the prospectuses in front of her and sighed. "Yes, I should appreciate what

I've already got with Owen and just concentrate on getting *this* right. It's kind of weird to think that possibly the rest of my working life could be decided in the next few weeks. That whatever I decide to put down on my UCAS form will map out my future career. It's kind of scary when you look at it like that, isn't it?"

"I... er, I guess so," faltered Kerry, disappointed that the conversation had swung back this way again.

"You don't sound too sure," Sonja pressed. "You're not having second thoughts about getting into primary teaching, are you?"

"Oh, no," Kerry shuffled uneasily in her seat. "Or at least, not really."

"Kerry, either you are or you're not."

"It's cool. I'll get it sorted," Kerry waffled, unwilling to mention to Sonja the thoughts that were going on in her head. Not till she was sure what they were herself.

"But Kez, these forms are supposed to be in soon..."

"I know. It's fine."

Kerry stifled a yawn and stretched her hands above her head lazily as though to emphasise the lack of urgency she felt towards the matter.

Sonja shook her head resignedly. "I don't know how you can be so laid-back about it all.

These are our futures we're talking about. Aren't you interested?"

"'Course," Kerry shrugged.

"Hmmm..."

Being as ambitious as she was, Sonja couldn't see how anyone could be so non-committal about their future. Especially when Sonja herself was champing at the bit to get on with it.

OK, so she was dithering a little over exactly which *type* of course to take, but she knew pretty much where she wanted to be in five years time. Namely, in a good media job in some big city, with a company car, nice flat and loads of disposable income.

She found Kerry's 'wait and see' attitude irritating, but instead of pressing the issue, she stuck her nose into her pile of prospectuses and said no more on the subject.

Kerry, meanwhile, stared vacantly out of the window once again. What Sonja didn't understand was that the last thing she wanted to think about was upping sticks and leaving Winstead and, more importantly, Ollie. The thought of going away tore her heart out.

Suddenly, Kerry's attention was caught by the sight of Matt and Gabrielle heading towards the café through the late afternoon gloom. She studied their faces.

Matt's was animated, all bright and smiley as he gesticulated with his arms as though trying to put across a point. Gabrielle, on the other hand, looked uncertain, her face troubled, her eyes studying the pavement as she walked. They made a weird picture, Kerry thought, like a couple at odds, rather than in love.

They came into the café and slipped into the seats next to Kerry and Sonja.

"You two looked deep in conversation when you were coming along the road..." said Kerry tentatively.

"I've been trying to persuade Gabrielle to come to the golf club dinner dance next Saturday. My old man's helped to organise it," Matt said brightly.

Sonja pulled a face. "And, understandably, Gabrielle has thought of some important reasons not to – like she's cutting her toenails that night, or watching her hair grow."

"Er... something like that," Gabrielle grimaced at her. "I mean, I'm sure it'll be a really posh do, I just think it sounds like the sort of thing old people go to."

"Too right, Gaby," Sonja shot her a sympathetic look. "What are you doing, Matt – trying to bore her to death?"

Matt looked hurt.

"It won't be so bad," he shrugged. "I've got to do the music—"

"Hip-hop and drum'n'bass, is it?" Sonja interrupted.

"The golden sounds of the sixties, actually," Matt corrected her, aware that he was being teased horribly. "It's just that it would be brilliant if Gaby could keep me company."

The girls looked unconvinced.

"But couldn't you take her along when you're DJing at something a bit more trendy, Matt?" Kerry suggested.

"Well, there's more to it than that. I just thought it would be a good time for Gabrielle to meet my dad properly. You know, get to know him a bit better," Matt tried to explain. "They've only ever said hello in passing."

"Ooh, *scary*," Sonja joked. "Sounds serious to me."

"Don't listen to them," Matt cajoled a dubious-looking Gabrielle. "Say you'll come. For me."

He looked pleadingly down at her and gave her a little kiss on the forehead.

"Oh, OK then," Gabrielle smiled back at him. "But if *one* person tries to speak to me about golf, you've got to rescue me straightaway – or you're chucked."

"That's my girl," Matt grinned, kissing her again.

He couldn't have looked any happier if she'd just agreed to marry him.

CHAPTER 4

• •

SWEET CINDERS

Cat unwrapped the pink towel from her head and moved a little closer to her dressing table mirror. She peered at the results of her hard work.

Hmmm, not a bad effort, she thought to herself as she pulled a comb through her hair.

She took her hairdryer from the top drawer and blow-dried her now muted blonde hair (from brassy to subtle, and minus the burgundy streaks) straight and neat and girlish. She was glad she hadn't had it cut in a while: it now fell down past her shoulders, and for some reason looked longer still when she swept it back with the blue velvet Alice band she'd just bought.

Cat studied her face and got ready to apply the 'no make-up' look. She'd practised it on plenty of people at college – just never on herself. With just a dash of mascara and eyeliner, and lips painted in Nearly Natural, she felt strangely naked, not having worn so little on her face in years.

Unable to resist a second coat of lipstick, Cat reapplied it to make the colour slightly more intense, then stood up and assessed the whole picture.

Definitely not me, she thought, *which is good, I suppose, if I'm trying to get into the part.*

Leaning towards the mirror with the most sweetly innocent expression on her face, she murmured, "Don't worry, Cinders, you *shall* go to the ball," then turned and left her room.

Cat was super-confident about landing the lead role in the panto. The Nativity play aside, she knew she could act – she sometimes felt that her whole life was one big performance. She was always adopting different personae depending on what situation she was in at the time, and she often wondered who the real Catrina Osgood was.

All she had to do for this part was psych herself up for the role of the gushingly good Cinderella, even though the character was so far removed from her own as to be a joke. But Cat knew she could pull it off.

Well, Jeff was impressed with my reading, she reassured herself, remembering the look of surprise on the lecturer's face as she'd breezed through the lines. *Now if I can just show the other lead actors in this rehearsal tonight that I can cut it, the part'll be mine...*

As she headed through town to the college, her mind was so focused on the task ahead that she didn't notice Sonja and Kerry approaching. Not until they were standing in front of her blocking her path.

"Cat! What's wrong?" Kerry asked, her brow furrowed with concern. "Are you feeling OK?"

"Huh?" Cat retorted, jerking her head up from the pavement she was staring intently at. "Oh, hi, guys. Uh... I feel fine. What d'you mean?"

"You look completely washed out," commented Sonja. "Drained, even."

Then the penny dropped. The others weren't used to seeing Cat with anything less than the entire Boots 17 make-up range caked on her face. No wonder they thought she looked sick.

"Oh, *this*," she exclaimed, raising her hand to her face and lightly touching her skin. "It's just something I'm trying out for Cinderella's make-up in the panto. What do you think?"

"Um, nice," Sonja said dubiously. "But aren't you taking your job too seriously? You're meant to put the make-up on the actress playing the part, not yourself!"

"Oh, *ha* ha, very funny. Actually..."

Cat stopped herself from saying any more. She suddenly realised she didn't want the others to know what she was up to. Not if there was the chance she might end up with a huge box of eggs liberally splattered over her face.

No, best she keep quiet about this little adventure; anyway, they'd only rib her if she did let on. She thought fast.

"...uh, what I mean is, the girl playing Cinderella can't make rehearsals tonight, so I'm helping out by reading her part."

"And you thought it would help you get into the role by looking like her, did you?" Sonja asked, an amused smile on her face.

"Yeah, well, why not? Seeing as I'm in charge of the make-up, I thought it would be a good opportunity to practise."

"Oh, right. But aren't you supposed to put *more* make-up on for this type of thing, rather than less?" Sonja quizzed. "Won't Cinders' face just be a blur from the third row back?"

"Not when it's only a rehearsal," Cat replied, exasperated by the probing questions, and desperately trying to come up with a feasible reply. "Obviously it'll be a lot heavier on the night. This is just to experiment with the *type* of look. Don't you know *anything* about the theatre, Sonja?"

"Obviously not," said Sonja, smothering a grin. "Obviously you're the expert – the girl who thinks she can get a career as the next soap queen by doing a beauty therapy course."

Catrina opened her mouth to say something cutting in reply, then closed it again. Bickering with her cousin wasn't on, not when she was trying to get in the right frame of mind for her meeting with the director and the cast.

Mellow out, Cat, she scolded herself. *Try and be nice. Cinderella would be.*

"You're right, Sonja." Cat simpered instead. "I am a silly thing, aren't I? To think I could ever really be someone special..."

There, that's better, she thought. *Could be a line right out of the panto.*

"Are you taking the mick?" asked Sonja, who'd instantly regretted her dig about Cat's career choice until this last sarky remark.

"N-n-no," Cat stuttered, "I'm just trying to be nice."

"Why?" Sonja demanded. "It's not your style to be nice, Cat. Kerry's *nice*. Joe's *nice*. 'Nice' isn't something you're really known for. What's up?"

Cat was taken aback. This wasn't going at all well.

She wondered what Cinderella would do in a situation like this, when she was being berated by one of the Ugly Sisters. *Probably carry on sweeping the floor,* she thought.

Kerry, meanwhile, stood with a bemused expression on her face. Cat was behaving oddly, for sure, but it didn't take much to rile Sonja where her cousin was involved. She decided now was the time to butt in on the feuding cousins.

"Come on, Son, let's go," she urged, "or we'll be late for the start of the film."

"Oh, are you going to the pictures? How lovely. I hope you have nice time," Cat trilled, batting her eyelashes girlishly from Kerry to Sonja and back again.

"God, there you go with that word again!" Sonja pointed out. "*Nice.*"

"Oh, I'm really sorry," Cat bleated and, remembering a line from the panto, added, "I didn't mean to upset you. Please forgive me, sweet sister, and I'll try to do better."

Chuffed that she could run a line or two off pat like that, Cat ended by giving a little skip and a hop towards Sonja and clasped her hands together in a pleading fashion. Just as she would to one of the Ugly Sisters on the big night. If she got the part.

Sonja looked at her cousin as if she was barking mad.

"I don't know what you're up to, Cat," she

sighed, "but for one thing, I'm not your sister, and for another, you're doing my head in."

She side-stepped Cat and turned to Kerry.

"Come on, Kez," she commanded. "Let's leave Miss Goody-Two-Shoes here to it. We've got a blood 'n' guts action movie to see."

Sonja set off up the road, a baffled-looking Kerry trailing in her wake.

"Have a lovely time! Hope it's not too gory!" Cat called after them.

She was off to her own battle zone. She was about to slay 'em as Cinderella...

CHAPTER 5

● ●

BREAK A LEG!

Cat's radar was in top gear when she arrived at college. There, in the corridor outside the main hall, she spotted the boys she had to impress tonight – both the Ugly Sisters and Prince Charming.

Ben and Jason (the sisters) were leaning against the wall, wearing for the moment the very un-ugly outfits of jeans and T-shirts. Glenn Wright, who was playing the Prince, was sitting with his back to her. Beside him sat a girl whose name Cat couldn't remember; a girl who was playing one of the villagers in a crowd scene.

Even from a distance, Cat could make out that they were running through lines.

As she walked over to them, the group all stopped talking and turned, as one, to look at her.

The new, toned-down Cat obviously took them by surprise.

"Hello, boys. Hello, er..." she trailed off, still lost as to the girl's name. "Have you come to cheer me on?"

Cat's tone was as bright and breezy as she could manage, even though her heart was hammering with nerves she wouldn't acknowledge. It was going to be hard charming these guys, she suddenly realised. The three boys hadn't been particularly friendly to her so far, treating her very much as a second-class citizen since she was 'just' the make-up girl and not a performer.

They're not exactly going to welcome me with open arms, she thought to herself. *They'll probably think I've got a cheek trying to have a go at acting...*

"Yeah, we heard you were having a bash at the lead role," Glenn smirked. "We can't wait to see what you can do."

More than you expect, you smarmy geek, she thought rebelliously.

"Great!" she beamed, adopting her sweet Cinderella guise. "I'm looking forward to it myself. And I'm especially looking forward to playing opposite you on the big night, Glenn," she added.

"You sound like it's already in the bag," Glenn laughed with a sarcastic undertone.

"Well, it is, isn't it?" replied Cat, all wide-eyed and girlish. "Jeff isn't going to find anyone else at this late stage. And I do know all the lines."

"You haven't heard about Amy then?" Jason butted in, nodding over at the girl beside Glenn.

"Amy?" Cat smiled, hoping the uncertainty over what was coming next wasn't apparent in her face.

"Amy's asked Jeff if she can have try-out tonight too," Glenn continued. "We're just running through her lines now."

The four faces – Glenn, Amy, Ben and Jason – all wore the same mocking expression as they waited for Cat's response.

Surprise and disappointment hit Cat like a tonne of bricks. She hadn't expected to face competition for the part; she'd assumed it was hers for the taking. But, like the natural actress she knew she was, she didn't let it show, and kept the smile glued to her face.

Anyway, she thought, as the thrill of the challenge sent a shiver through her, *it'll be more of a pleasure than ever to see the smug looks wiped off their arrogant faces.*

"Glad to hear it," she cooed in Amy's direction. "Break a leg!"

43

Four pairs of eyes watched in amazement as she padded away confidently in her blue suede ballet pumps. There was absolutely no external clue to show just how literally Cat had meant that last remark!

• • •

"I didn't know Amy was going to try for the part."

"She only approached me about it this morning, Catrina," Jeff replied, turning his attention away from the props that were being set up on the stage. "You're all right about it, aren't you?"

"Oh, yes!" she nodded. "She's one of the drama students, so of *course* you have to give her a go."

"That's very understanding of you," said Jeff. "But it doesn't mean I'm not going to give you a fair hearing, Catrina, if you still want to go ahead..."

"Of course I do!" trilled Cat. "So, how are we going to work this?"

"Well, I thought Amy could have a bash at the opening scene..."

Damn! thought Cat. *I wanted to be first on and make my big impression.*

"...and then you take over in scene two. Then

we'll keep alternating between you as we run through. OK?"

"Fine," smiled Cat.

She turned and made her way to the side door that led to the wings. She wanted to watch Amy's performance from these darkened partitions so no one could see her face if Amy happened to be brilliant.

Which she isn't *going to be*. Cat tried to psych herself up, as her rival, the Ugly Sisters and the Wicked Stepmother made their way forward on to the stage.

"Jeff will cast Amy, won't he?" she suddenly heard someone say in the shadows close by.

"Definitely! He'd never risk giving it to that blonde bimbo from the beauty course..." she heard someone else reply.

Cat felt her bottle go. Even though out on stage she could see that Amy was reading from a script that she hadn't yet memorised, it didn't give her any pleasure. The realisation that too many people were there to snigger at her rather than applaud her – who'd love to see her come a cropper – made the task ahead seem impossible.

"Don't pay any attention," a voice whispered in her ear. "They're just being morons."

Beside Cat stood Vikki Grant, the larger than life black girl who was determined to play the most over-the-top Fairy Godmother that any Cinderella had ever had.

Vikki was Cat's favourite person to make up in the cast; she had demanded that Cat go mad with the glitter, to be in keeping with her amazing pink net confection of a costume. And after the offhand way Glenn and some of the others talked to her when they were sitting in front of the make-up mirror, it was always a pleasure to hear Vikki's throaty laugh and have a giggle with her.

"Thanks, Vikki" smiled Cat, some of her confidence seeping back at the girl's kind words.

"So, do you know the lines or are you going to read off the script like madam?" Vikki nodded her head towards Amy.

"I know them off by heart."

"Good," whispered Vikki. "Well, you've got one over her for a start. Just get up there and belt 'em out. And remember – it's a panto; you can go overboard if you want to. Which is what too many of this bunch of precious ac*torrrs* seem to be forgetting."

Cat studied Amy's well-acted but very subtle style and knew Vikki was right. That performance wasn't going to hold any audience's interest for an hour and a half.

"Go get 'em!" whispered Vikki, as the first

scene ended and it was Cat's turn to step on to the stage.

"Don't worry, I will..." growled Cat with a determined glint in her eye.

● ● ●

Cat gulped the water from the plastic cup and hoped it would cool her down quickly. Apart from feeling so hot, her head was thudding now the rehearsal was finished – though whether it was from belting out the songs or because of the improvised dance steps she'd done at the same time, Cat didn't know.

What she *did* know was that she'd done the best she could. Amy's performance – reading from the script aside – was confident and assured. Cat's had been like an explosion in a fireworks factory, with no one, including Cat, sure of what was coming next.

"Well done, Cat," came Jeff's voice as he appeared at her side. "That was a very, uh, spirited effort. You did a really good job under the circumstances. Thank you."

"So – have I got the part?" Cat blurted out.

Jeff stroked his chin thoughtfully before he answered.

"Why don't I give you a call some time

tomorrow?" he said evasively, putting his hand on her shoulder and steering her out of the hall and out of earshot of the others. "We can discuss it in more detail then."

That's it, Cat thought despondently as she padded along the echoing corridor. *That's just a nice way of saying thanks-but-no-thanks. I've blown it.*

CHAPTER 6

● ●

OH YES HE IS?

It was late by the time Sonja got home from the cinema. The rest of her family seemed to be in bed which was where Sonja heading as soon as she'd made herself a coffee.

As she got to her bedroom, she saw a bright pink Post-it note stuck to the door.

Owen called, it said. *Ring any time before midnight.*

Sonja felt her insides give a little jolt of pleasure. She loved it when Owen called out of the blue like this. They had an unspoken agreement where they usually talked once every week or so, often late in the evening, and usually about nothing in particular – they just liked hearing the sound of each other's voices.

Sonja looked at her watch.

Eleven thirty. Perfect, just perfect.

She went into her room, closed the door quietly behind her and picked up the extension by the side of her bed. She tapped in the number that was imprinted on her brain and listened to the dialling tone at the other end, her insides fluttering in nervous excitement.

It took eleven rings for Owen to answer the phone. When he did, his voice sounded husky, as though he hadn't spoken to anyone for days.

"It's me," Sonja said. "I didn't get you out of bed, did I?"

"Sonja, hi. No, I was vegging in front of the telly. Must've dozed off. How're things?"

"Great. I've just got back from the flicks with Kerry. We went to see this dreadful Keanu Reeves film. It was hilarious, I can't tell you how bad it was. Everyone was laughing in all the wrong places it was so terrible."

"I've heard about that one," Owen said. "It's had awful reviews. Why on earth did you go and see it?"

"Because Kerry used to fancy him and there was nothing else on. I guess we'd have been better off staying at home and watching *Family Fortunes*."

"Yeah, I'm sure you're right. And Les Dennis is so much hunkier than Keanu Reeves, isn't he?"

Sonja laughed. "So what were you calling me for anyway?"

"Do I need to call you for a reason now?" Owen teased her.

"No, of course not!" said Sonja, pretending to be hurt.

"Well, anyway, I spoke to Anna the other night and she said you'd been missing me..."

"I did not say that!" Sonja protested.

"What, you mean you *haven't* been missing me?"

"Of course I have," giggled Sonja, realising she'd backed herself into a corner. "So, will I be seeing you again soon?"

"I have to say work hasn't exactly been generous with the holidays – we've got this big contract coming up right at the beginning of January."

"That's OK," said Sonja, trying to sound like an undemanding and understanding girlfriend. If girlfriend was what she actually was.

"Oh, sorry – told you I was half asleep," Owen apologised as he gave a yawn. "But actually Anna asked me to come for Christmas..."

Sonja felt a surge of emotion while Owen lost himself in another involuntary yawn. She'd been wondering whether Owen might come and visit Anna for a few days over the Christmas holiday, but hardly dared hope that he really would. And now it was true!

Just as she was about to ask when he would arrive, a voice cut in on the line.

"Oh, sorry," came Lottie's voice from one of the other extensions. "I didn't mean to interrupt you lovebirds."

"Well, shut up and wait your turn, will you?" said Sonja, irritated by her sister's interruption.

"Yeah, but do us a favour and make it quick. I've got to catch my mate before it gets too late."

"*Yes*, OK," intoned Sonja in a bored drawl.

A short click followed and she found herself alone – miles apart – with Owen once again.

"Yeah, what was I saying?" Owen bumbled sleepily. "Oh, yeah, Anna had said that Mum could go to our aunt's for once so she wouldn't be on her own, then I said—"

The phone line clicked into life again and Lottie's voice became three's company. "Finished yet?"

"No!" snapped Sonja. "Just give us a minute!"

The line clicked silent.

"That's a great idea, Owen!" Sonja picked up from where they'd left off, hardly able to contain her excitement at his news.

He's coming! she thought. *This is the best Christmas present ever.*

"So you don't mind?" came the slightly puzzled reply.

"No, not at all. Why would I mind?" Sonja giggled.

A click cut through.

"If I could get a turn on the phone any time this century, that would be good..." tried Lottie, still light-hearted but evidently more than a little fed up now.

"Oh, listen, I'm going to have to go, Owen," Sonja apologised, while mentally making a note to ask her parents if they'd consider getting an extra line put in. "I'll talk to you later, yeah?"

"Later..." came the sleepy voice so far away.

As soon as the receiver was down, Sonja punched the air and hissed "Yes!" at her reflection in the mirror on top of the chest of drawers.

Owen was coming. She felt like she'd just won the Lottery.

CHAPTER 7

●●●●●●●●●●●●●●●●●●●●●●●●●●●●●

FAIRY TALE ENDING?

Cat was in a foul mood. Since the night before she had been on an emotional roller-coaster ride, from supremely confident to desperately disappointed, and at every stop in between. One day on and she was convinced she'd made a complete fool of herself.

At the time, she'd thought she'd given a pretty unforgettable performance – but if she had, why hadn't Jeff offered her the part on the spot? It was obvious now that that stupid Amy girl was going to get it instead. And, in the meantime, Cat would be a laughing stock for weeks to come. The make-up girl who'd had ideas above her station.

How very Cinderella, huffed Cat. *Only I don't get the happy ending.*

Now, as she arrived home after a rotten day at

college – most of which was spent avoiding anyone involved with the Drama Department – she was feeling very angry with the world. When she got to the third-floor flat of the smart mansion block she lived in, Cat hoped her mum was still at work, as she often was at this time of day. She didn't want to have to make polite conversation with her, not when she felt as down as this.

Cat put her key in the lock, threw open the door, banging it against the wall, and slammed it shut again.

"Keep the noise down, will you?" she heard her mother shout from the living room. "I'm trying to go through some figures for work."

Damn! thought Cat. *Oh, well, just because she's here doesn't mean I have to speak to her.*

Cat kicked off her shoes and thumped noisily towards the kitchen.

"Oh, there was a message for you on the answering machine, but I accidentally wiped it off," her mother called out.

"Oh, for God's sake, that's all I need," Cat muttered. "On top of everything else that's bad in my life, I've got a senile, deranged mother who doesn't know how to use the answering machine."

"Who was it from?" she shouted back, her

head stuck in the fridge looking for juice. The fridge was virtually bare, apart from a carton of organic yoghurt and a wrinkled cucumber.

"Add to that the fact that she's *sooo* busy she can't even be bothered to shop for food," Cat hissed, slamming the fridge shut and heading towards her room.

"Some guy called Jeff," Sylvia Osgood called. "Said something about you ringing him at home tonight."

Cat flew into the living room.

"*What?*" she demanded. "What else did he say?"

"Sorry, Catrina," her mother said, not looking up from her computer. "Like I said, I wiped the message. He sounded quite old though. He's not a boyfriend, is he?"

"Don't be so stupid, Mum. Of course he isn't! Did he leave his number?"

"Uh, yes, but I didn't make a note of it. Was it important?"

Cat was livid. "Oh, *no*, Mum. It was only possibly the most important phone call I'm ever likely to get in my life – and you wiped the number. I can't *believe* you could be so stupid!"

For the first time since the conversation had started, Sylvia turned from her work and looked sternly at her daughter.

"Now look here, madam," she said, her voice

icy cold, "that's enough of your cheek. I said I was sorry. If you weren't out gallivanting around town quite so much you might be in a position to pick up your own messages. As it is, you'll have to rely on your stupid mother who also lines your pockets with a rather hefty allowance every month. Now, you don't want me to put a stop to that part of your life, do you?"

Cat bit her tongue. Any mention of having her allowance stopped always sent her back-peddling; the thought of having to get a part-time job to supplement her lifestyle was appalling to someone who dedicated herself to having a good time as much as she did.

Instead, she picked up the phone, dialled 1471 and waited to hear the recorded message. The last call had been received nearly an hour ago. The number wasn't local and while Cat knew Jeff lived out of town, she had no idea where.

She figured she had nothing to lose by dialling. She could always pretend it was a wrong number if the person on the other end didn't know what she was going on about.

Cat punched in the digits and listened intently as it rang. Finally, a woman answered the phone.

"Hello?"

"Hello? Could I speak to Jeff please?"

"Who's calling?"

Phew, must be the right place. "Uh, it's Catrina Osgood."

"Just a minute, I'll get him for you."

Cat sat on the edge of her chair and drummed her nails nervously on the table. She could hear her heart pounding in her chest as she waited for what seemed like several aeons before he came to the phone.

"Hello?"

"Jeff, hi, it's Catrina Osgood," she said as lightly as possible. "I'm returning your call from earlier..."

"Ah, yes, Catrina," he said vaguely as though he was scratching his head trying to think why he'd rung her in the first place.

She visualised his messy mop of greying hair and absently decided she'd offer him a free haircut if he gave her the part. Fat chance...

"I hoped to catch you at college today, but we must have missed each other. I was ringing to let you know that I've thought long and hard about your, erm, performance..."

He paused to cough loudly.

Come on, get on with it! Cat felt like shouting down the line.

"...Excuse me," he continued, "bit of a cough. Uh, like I was saying, I thought your read-through was robust..."

Robust, Cat fretted. *Is that good or bad?*

"...and although I believe we'll have our work cut out to get ready in time for the performance, I'd like to offer you the part. Of Cinderella, that is."

"Yesss!" yelped Cat, immediately picturing what new style she'd cut Jeff's hair into.

"It means lots of work, Catrina," he tried to reaffirm.

"I don't care!"

"We're going to have to have plenty of extra coaching sessions and mini-rehearsals."

"No problemo!"

"What?" asked Jeff dubiously.

"Er, that'll be fine," Cat calmed herself enough to say. She was, after all, Cinderella.

And Cinderella most certainly never came out with "no problemo".

• • •

Sonja was desperate to see Anna. She had hardly slept the night before, she was so pumped up by the prospect of Owen coming to stay.

She had loads of pre-Christmas plans for them and she wanted to include Anna as much as possible. After all, if it wasn't for her, they'd never have met.

As soon as sixth form was over for the day, she and Kerry sped off to the End.

"I hope Anna doesn't want him the whole time he's down here, though," Sonja mused as they hurried along the road. "I mean, it would be nice if I could have him to myself for a tiny little while."

"How long is he coming down for?" Kerry asked.

"I don't know. We never got that far into the conversation. Lottie was getting on my nerves interrupting every two seconds, so I said I'd catch him later."

"Yeah, right," Kerry giggled, raising her eyes knowingly. "Well, I'm sure you'll be able to get him to yourself at some point over Christmas, even if it's just a quick smacker under the mistletoe."

They were at the café now; Sonja went bounding inside and straight up to the counter where Anna was pouring out hot chocolate drinks for customers.

"Hi, Anna," Sonja beamed. "Isn't it great news about Owen?"

"What's that then?" Anna asked, a quizzical look on her face.

"You *know*, about him coming to Winstead for Christmas. He told me last night..."

Anna looked blankly at Sonja for a moment,

then her eyes lit up as she took in what had just been said.

"You're kidding!" she said incredulously. "You mean he's coming down after all?"

"Yes!" laughed Sonja, stamping her feet in excitement.

"Wow," nodded Anna, one empty cup still held, forgotten, in mid-air. "When I last spoke to him he said he was definitely going to Mum's for Christmas!"

"Yeah, that's right, he did mention something about that," Sonja said vaguely, waving her hand around, "but he said he was coming here instead."

"Sonja, that's brilliant!"

"Isn't it?" giggled Sonja.

Anna felt a rush of comfort flood over her. Christmas wasn't going to be a lonely, hollow day after all: she was going to have her wonderful brother with her. Even if she would have to share him.

"You know, I thought if anyone would be able to swing it, *you* could," said Anna, oblivious to the customers who were now looking over restlessly for their drinks. "When we talked a couple of days ago, he was adamant that he was going home to Mum. I *thought* he sounded keener on coming here once I reminded him he'd be able to see you as well, but he still seemed determined to go home. I can't believe he's changed his mind! What else did he say?"

"Not a lot. We got interrupted by my sister. I don't even know what day he's arriving."

"I'll call him later on and let you know. It'll be brilliant, we'll all have a great time."

"You don't mind me butting in occasionally then?" Sonja grinned.

"Not at all, Son. I'm relying on you to get all the parties lined up."

"I was hoping you'd say that."

"Let me get these things out of the way then I'll come over and take your order. On the house."

"Cheers, Anna." Sonja went over to the table in the window where Kerry was now sitting with Matt, Gabrielle and Joe.

"So, Son," Matt grinned. "We hear lover boy's coming to stay. No wonder you're bouncing about like you've got ants in your pants."

"That's great news," added Gabrielle. "I bet you can't wait."

"You're not wrong, Gaby." Sonja slid into the banquette next to Kerry. "I kind of hoped he would come down, but now I know it's really happening, I'm dead excited."

"Aw, it's really sweet," Gabrielle continued.

"Yeah, just make sure you invite us all to the wedding," smirked Matt.

"Oh, ha bloomin' ha," Sonja shot back. "I think you and Gabrielle will be heading up the aisle before I do."

Matt looked away almost bashfully and gave Gabrielle's hand a little squeeze.

"You never know," he teased, "we might just surprise you, mightn't we, Gab?"

Gabrielle gave a shy smile and pulled her hand away. "Um, well, considering I'm still only fourteen, I don't think anyone should start looking for posh new frocks yet!" she laughed, almost nervously.

"So how was your film last night?" Joe asked Sonja and Kerry, changing the subject.

"A stinker," Sonja replied. "One to be avoided at all costs. Kerry and I had more fun discussing Cat's latest antics than the film."

"What do you mean?" frowned Joe.

"Well, we bumped into her on the way to one of her panto rehearsals and she was acting really weirdly, wasn't she, Kez?"

Kerry nodded. "She certainly didn't seem to be her usual self."

"What, you mean she didn't have her broomstick with her?" Matt sniggered.

"Matt! That's really mean," Gabrielle exclaimed, bashing him on the arm. "She's not so bad."

"Oh, come on," he objected, grinning, "she can be a right old witch when she wants to. You just think she's OK because you haven't experienced a Catrina Osgood tongue-lashing yet. You wait till you get on the wrong side of her, then you'll know what I mean."

"Well, that's just it," Sonja continued. "When we saw her, she went from being the same old Cat we love to hate to a complete wet blanket. And all in the space of five minutes. It was dead spooky, wasn't it, Kez?"

"Yeah and she was wearing hardly any make-up," Kerry added, "which made her look even spookier."

"Maybe she's going for a revamp," suggested Matt. "She's always changing her 'look'. I'm waiting for the day her hair drops out."

"I dunno about that, but something strange is going on," Sonja said, narrowing her eyes. "And I bet it's got something to do with a guy."

"Maybe she's planning on getting to know Prince Charming a lot better!" Kerry joked, without realising just how right she was.

CHAPTER 8

● ●

FIRST-NIGHT NERVES

"So how's Ollie feeling at this moment?" Matt asked Kerry. "Is he panicking yet?"

Leaning back in his seat at the café, Matt chuckled to himself at the vision he had in his mind of his friend's current state. It was Thursday evening and The Loud were about to play their first weekly gig at the Railway Tavern. The band were already there, setting up their equipment, while the rest of their supporters (which consisted at this moment of Kerry, Matt, Maya and Sonja) were meeting at the café before going on to the gig later.

"Actually, the only thing he's panicking about is where you are," Kerry responded. "You're supposed to be in charge of their sound mixing, aren't you?"

Kerry had just left Ollie at the Railway Tavern and walked to the café to join her friends, her face pale with worry at the thought of the upcoming gig. She had left Ollie surprisingly cool about it all, unlike Kerry who had already made several trips to the loo and felt quite nervous at the prospect of what lay ahead. Although she'd seen them play loads of times before, it didn't stop Kerry from getting jittery – much more so than Ollie who took most of it in his stride.

"Yes, it's all set up," Matt tried to explain himself. "I was just waiting here to meet Gabrielle so she wouldn't have to walk into the pub on her own."

"Well, we're all here waiting for her. You don't have to oversee her every movement," Sonja teased him. "Who are you – her dad?"

"Very funny," said Matt, who showed no sign of moving, preferring instead to make sure his girlfriend arrived safe and sound. He glanced at his watch. "Maybe I should have gone and picked her up..."

"Oh, shut up, Matt," Sonja groaned. "So what about Joe and Billy and Andy? How were they doing nerve-wise?"

"Billy and Andy seem fine. Joe's gone a bit quiet."

"Poor Joe..." sympathised Maya.

Joe wasn't the most confident of people. It was just as well he played drums and could hide away behind his kit and the rest of the band.

"I think he's a bit like me. He worries too much about what might go wrong," Kerry sighed. "And the more often he plays, the more problems he thinks of."

"What about Nick?" Matt asked. "He was swanning about like a proud father when I was there earlier."

"Well, he's been really good, y'know? Like a proper manager," said Kerry. "Getting them organised and making sure no one's going to bottle out at the last minute."

"At least it's not their first-ever gig," Maya said. "They must be pretty confident about how it's going to turn out. When they played at The Bell a few weeks back they were brilliant. Everyone said so. They ought to be encouraged by that."

Sonja nodded in agreement. "Yeah, and that guy Derek from the Railway Tavern must have liked them or he wouldn't have booked them for this regular spot."

"I just hope it stays regular," Kerry frowned. "There aren't exactly people fighting to get in right now."

The four of them leant forward and peered out the window, down towards the Railway Tavern next door to the old Victorian station buildings. An old guy and his dog seemed to pause at the door; but as soon as the dog had cocked its leg, they moved on.

And that appeared to be the only action happening along there at the moment.

"Don't look so tense, Kerry. It'll be fine," Sonja said soothingly, registering the concern on her friend's face. "I'll go and see if Anna's coming too, so we increase the numbers a bit."

Sonja went up to the serving counter and peered into the kitchen beyond. She knew Anna must be around somewhere and she was keen to talk to her about Owen.

"Hello?" Sonja called out. "Anna? Are you in there?"

Anna's head popped out from behind an enormous fridge.

"Be with you in a tick, Sonja," she called. "I'm just putting some of this stuff away for the night."

When she re-emerged she rubbed her hands together in an effort to warm them up and came back into the café.

"Hi," Sonja beamed. "Have you spoken to Owen yet?"

"No, I've been trying ever since last evening. But there's no reply and he hasn't got his answering machine on either. I don't like to call him at work, not with it being a new job and him being so busy. I can't imagine where he is."

"He's probably out celebrating Christmas early. He'll be all partied out by the time he gets to Winstead."

"I doubt it, not Owen. Not with the workload he's been moaning about," Anna smiled. "Have you got some parties lined up for him when he arrives?"

"Yeah, loads. His feet won't touch the ground once he gets here," laughed Sonja. "And I've had an absolutely brilliant idea too..."

She broke off, not sure how Anna would react to her plan.

"Go on," Anna said.

"*Well*, I know we don't know what day he's coming down yet, but I thought, wouldn't it be great if you had a little 'welcome home' type party at your flat the night he gets here? Or at least a 'welcome back to Winstead' do. What do you think?"

"Mmm, that's sounds lovely," nodded Anna, savouring the notion of making her tiny flat upstairs spring to life with lights and laughter and friends. "We could make it a surprise. Maybe I'll tell him he can't get here until a certain time in the evening and when he walks in we'll all be there waiting for him. He'd love it!"

"Brilliant!"

Both girls grabbed each other's hands and squealed excitedly.

"Of course, it couldn't be a big do," Anna continued. "You can't get that many people in my flat. But we could invite all of the gang, and Nick and anyone else who's got to know him."

"I can't wait!" said Sonja dreamily.

"Yeah, but if you get through to him on the phone before I do, be careful you don't let slip about this."

"'Course not! Oh, Anna – I'm so pleased he's coming, it's going to be the best Christmas ever for me."

"Same here, Son. I don't mind admitting it now, but I was in for a pretty miserable time until yesterday. I didn't have a thing planned. Now we've both got loads to look forward to. It's going to be great!"

Sonja gave Anna a look of sisterly concern.

"You know, Anna, you need to get out more. It doesn't do you any good being stuck here all day and most of the night. You'll have to have a word with Nick in the New Year, get yourself some more time off... You're coming to the gig at the Tavern tonight, aren't you?"

Anna smiled. She found Sonja's concern sweet. She already felt that the gang had accepted her as one of their own, but this made her feel even more as if she finally belonged.

"Yeah, I wouldn't miss it for the world."

"Great. Well, it looks like we're all off. I'll see you later."

Sonja rejoined the others who were getting their coats on ready to make the short walk to the pub, now that they'd spotted Gabrielle making her way towards the End.

"How are you feeling?" Sonja asked Kerry. "Still nervous?"

"A bit," she replied. "I'm sure I'll be fine once they come on. It's pathetic really; anyone would think it was me having to get up there on stage in front of everyone, not Ollie."

"They'll be great," Maya enthused, linking her arm with Kerry's. "I'm dead excited. I've never known anyone in a proper band before."

"You can go around telling everyone you're with the band," grinned Matt as he opened the door. "It's a great pulling line."

"Well, you'd know all about that, wouldn't you?" Sonja smirked. "It's a good job Gaby's got you in check or you'd be a complete nightmare tonight."

Matt put his arm protectively around Gabrielle's shoulder and pulled her towards him as she kissed him hello. Looking up at him, she gave him a little smile and he kissed her again on the top of the head.

"Ignore them," he whispered, giving her a little squeeze. "You know how I feel about you."

"You *are* coming tonight, aren't you, Anna?" Kerry asked as they walked past her as she finished cleaning a table.

"Yeah, but I won't finish up here until gone nine," she replied. "What time are they on?"

"About ten."

"OK, I'll see you all there."

The gang trooped out of the café and made their way noisily along the street to the less than sold-out gig.

CHAPTER 9

● ●

GREAT EXPECTATIONS

"Five minutes, lads."

Derek, the landlord of the Railway Tavern, poked his head around the door and gave them the thumbs up. Then he disappeared again, leaving Ollie, Joe, Billy and Andy in various stages of nervousness as they prepared for their performance.

Joe turned to the others and gave them a weak smile. His face was drained, even paler than normal, and his hands shook as he read through the band's running order for the hundredth time. He'd played live enough times before, but tonight felt important and worthy of more nerves than normal: if no one was interested in listening to The Loud, this nice little residency would soon be up the spout.

Constantly buttoning and unbuttoning the cuffs of his shirt, Billy paced the dressing room – which was difficult really, seeing as it doubled up as a store room. He only had to take a few strides from one side before he hit a pile of cardboard boxes or a fridge or a vacuum cleaner. He hummed the tune of their opening song relentlessly and repetitively as he walked.

Andy watched absent-mindedly from a chair and tuned and retuned his bass guitar, tapping his foot up and down on the stone floor to a melody inside his head.

Ollie pulled on his T-shirt and then sprawled across a decrepit sofa that had half its ancient stuffing spilling from a large hole to one side. He had his eyes shut and a peaceful look on his face. He seemed totally oblivious to the movement going on around him.

When he heard the door open again, he barely managed to open one eye to see who it was. When he realised it was only his Uncle Nick, he drifted off again, back to playing Wembley Stadium in his head.

"OK, lads, time to get moving," said Nick cheerfully, clapping his hands.

"Um, are there many people out there?" Andy asked.

"Don't worry, Andy," beamed Nick. "There are

enough to keep Derek happy, you can be sure of that. You boys just concentrate on blowing everyone away, eh? Are we all ready then?"

Ollie hauled himself out of his comfy position and joined his mates who were standing in an orderly line behind Nick. He exited through the door and strode along the dim corridor towards the stage.

The others followed meekly behind.

• • •

Anna hugged her coffee mug and took another bite of the cheese and ham toastie she'd made herself. Between wrapping up at the café for Nick and rushing to get herself changed and ready to go out to the gig, she didn't have time to eat anything more substantial.

Now, as the clock on the wall showed her it was nearly ten o'clock, it occurred to her to sneak in yet another quick call to Owen before she ran down to watch the band. She needed to know when he was arriving so that she could plan ahead for the surprise mini-party she and her friends were going to spring on him.

The phone rang and rang, unanswered.

Anna was beginning to get worried. Where was Owen? Why didn't his flatmate pick up the phone? Why wasn't the answering machine switched on?

Maybe someone else might know where he was. Anna took a deep breath and dialled their mother's number.

Shouldn't be too late, she thought to herself, glancing at the clock again.

She and her mother had spoken briefly on the phone a couple of times since her mother's visit to Winstead a few weeks back, but although they were trying to heal the rift between them, Anna found it hard work. She still preferred it when Owen acted as go-between.

Margaret Michaels answered the phone immediately and sounded pleased when she realised it was her daughter on the line. They chatted amicably for a few moments, before Anna finally got around to the real reason she was calling.

"Mum, I've been trying to contact Owen for days," she said, "but there's no reply. You don't know what he's up to, do you?"

"He's away on a training course," her mother explained.

"Oh, right. He never mentioned it. I was starting to get worried since no one ever seemed to be in."

"Well, I hear his flatmate is courting so hasn't

spent much time there recently. Owen's a right one for forgetting to switch that answering machine of his on. They didn't tell you where he was at work?"

"I didn't like to call him there, not with it being a new job and everything."

"Oh, I don't think they would mind too much," her mum replied confidently. "He's getting on very well by all accounts, and of course he loves it. But you probably already know that. Actually, Anna..."

She hesitated before carrying on.

"I was going to call you myself. I wondered if you'd be able to come home at all this Christmas? It would be lovely to see you, and Owen is coming for a few days so you'd have him for company. I know you've got your own flat and lots of friends, but even if you could only spare a day or so, it would be so lovely to see you, dear, it really would."

Anna was taken aback. What did she mean about Owen going home? Not according to Sonja he wasn't.

Then realisation struck Anna: Owen couldn't have *told* their mum he wasn't going home yet, just as he couldn't have told her that Anna wouldn't be visiting either. Anna didn't know what to say.

She suddenly felt sorry for her mother. She imagined her making all sorts of plans for the Michaels' Christmas family reunion, blissfully unaware that neither of her children were intending to spend it with her.

Calling me 'dear', for God's sake, after all she's called me in the past, Anna thought sadly.

"Anna? Are you still there?"

Anna had to think fast.

"Yes, I'm still here," she said quietly. "Uh, can you leave it with me for a day or so, Mum? I'm not sure what's happening with the café. My boss might be keeping it open for a lot of the holiday, in which case I'll have to work. I need the money. But as soon as I know, I'll call you. Promise. Is that OK?"

It was a lie, but it was all she could think of and her mother accepted the explanation with good grace. Anyway, Anna wasn't brutal enough to blurt out the truth. She needed to talk to Owen; they should decide between them the best way to handle this.

As Anna came off the phone she felt like the bad guy in a soap opera. She looked over at the clean clothes she'd just dug out to change into and realised miserably that she was in no mood to go out and be sociable now.

Because I'm going to have a good Christmas,

it means my mum's has to be full of disappointment, she worried guiltily.

Pulling her curtains closed, Anna wished with all her heart that Christmas could just be cancelled...

CHAPTER 10

● ●

DISTANT PUNTERS

The gang stood at the bar of the Railway Tavern taking in their surroundings. It wasn't the smartest place in the world – with its Formica-topped tables and fake brass lighting that had seen better days, it was certainly more of a dive than Ollie's parents' pub. The bar ran along one end of the pub, then the tables lined two walls, with the stage set up in one corner.

All the tables were occupied and there was a handful of people already congregating at the front of the stage, waiting for the band to come on. Kerry guessed there must be thirty or forty people there; not bad, but not brilliant either. At least the gang were there to support Ollie and the boys.

She was slightly bugged to see that Cat hadn't shown her face yet. Everyone else was there (apart from Anna who was probably rushing to get ready); and Cat had promised faithfully to come along.

But no sooner had she thought bad things about her, than Kerry saw Cat sweep through the pub towards them at great speed, an enormous grin on her face, and looking very different from the *au naturel* vision that Kerry and Sonja had encountered the previous evening.

Cat had piled her blonde hair on top of her head to give a messy bird's nest appearance, and her heavily made-up face was coloured in all shades of violet – lips, eyes and cheeks, with a liberal sprinkling of purple glitter to finish it off. She wore a fluffy, candyfloss cardie, held together across her chest by two large, heart-shaped clips, and skin-tight white pedal-pushers. Chunky white shoes finished the look off.

Subtle was not the word.

"Hey! Everyone! Listen! You'll never guess what!" she hollered as she bounded up to the group.

"What's that, Cat?" Maya asked, smiling at the bouncing vision in front of her.

"I'm gonna be in Cinderella! Me! Can you believe it?"

"Cinderella. Right," Matt said slowly. "Er, Cat, what are you talking about?"

Cat looked around the sea of confused faces and put one hand to her forehead in exasperation. How could they *not* understand what she was going on about?

"Cinderella," she repeated. "At Christmas. The college pantomime. You know, the one I've been doing the make-up for? Well, they've only offered me a part in the show. Me! Isn't it the best?"

"Cat, that's great for you," enthused Maya generously. "Erm, what sort of part is it?"

"An Ugly Sister, of course!" Matt snorted.

"Haven't you got to go and twiddle some knobs on that sound desk before the band starts?" Maya said sternly to Matt. "Ignore him, Cat. What part have you got?"

Catrina looked round at the group of faces staring at her – Sonja and Matt still sniggering at his stupid remark.

Suddenly, she decided that there was no way she was going to have the others mock what she was doing. It was hard enough knowing she'd have to win round most of the rest of the cast of the panto itself, without having to suffer silly jibes from her so-called mates.

Let's just see their faces on the night, she thought to herself, imagining her friends' stunned expressions when they saw her walk out on stage as the star of the show. Until then, she decided, she was keeping her true identity under wraps.

"It's no big deal; just a bit part in the crowd," she shrugged. "You probably won't even be able to see me..."

"Well, we won't bother coming then," Matt blundered tactlessly on, a dopey smile plastered across his face.

"Matt!" Gabrielle hissed at her boyfriend, before smiling over at Cat. "I'm looking forward to going. The profits are for charity, aren't they?"

"That's right," Cat nodded. "And I've got a wodge of tickets in my bag tonight which I'm hoping you'll all buy!"

"Of course," said Kerry, already rifling in her bag for money.

She needn't have hurried herself.

"Ooh, look!" Cat exclaimed. "Maya! Over there!"

"What?" asked Maya, peering into the shadowy recesses of the pub and trying to figure out what Cat was on about.

"Come on!" instructed Cat, still holding Maya's hand and trying to drag her across the pub.

"Cat, what is it?" Maya cried, confusion all over her face.

"It's the tasty boys! The ones who've been hanging around at the End. "You know, whass-theirnames? Rudi and Marc, the Swedish boys."

"Ah, yes, you mean the Dutch boys," Maya said, looking into the distance and finally picking out the two boys.

"Come on," Cat instructed. "Let's go and chat them up and see if I can flog them some tickets at the same time."

"What do you need me for?" asked Maya reluctantly. She knew the lads to say hello to, but that was as far as it went.

"Their English still isn't that hot. I need you as interpreter!"

"I can't speak Dutch!" Maya tried to argue.

As far as Maya could see, Cat's world-class flirting was bound to overcome any language barrier she might hit.

"Come on – you're the only really swotty friend I've got. Come and help me persuade them!" whined Cat.

With that dubious compliment, she pulled a reluctant Maya off in the direction of the two boys.

● ● ●

Kerry stood with the rest of the gang near the front of the stage and bit her lip anxiously. The Loud were a third of a way into their set and, so far, most of the people in the pub seemed more intent on downing their beer or talking to their mates than watching the band. Of the people listening to the music, the majority were kids who hung out at the End or people Kerry recognised from St Mark's sixth form.

She wanted to shout out to everyone to shut up and listen. Instead, she tried to overcompensate by dancing overenthusiastically to every track. It wasn't that the band were playing badly – they weren't – but they were having trouble getting everyone's attention.

So far, their set had consisted of mainly upbeat stuff – sort of Blur meets Supergrass – but, in a flash of inspiration after the fifth song and still no movement from the audience apart from Kerry's sterling efforts, Ollie turned to the others and motioned that they change the running order.

They took the pace right down and began a haunting ballad which started with just Andy on bass guitar and Ollie speaking the first few lines of the song.

The reaction from the audience was instant; a hush came over the place as people previously more interested in talking among themselves took notice of the band for the first time that evening.

Maya came over and touched Kerry's arm.

"I love this one," she sighed. "What is it again?"

"It's *Distant Lovers*," Kerry replied, then added ruefully, "remember?"

Maya nodded. "Ah, yes," she said, "of course."

It was a song Kerry wasn't overly fond of. A while back when she and Ollie hadn't been getting along so well, she had read the lyrics to it and mistakenly come to the conclusion that Ollie had written it about the love he felt for his ex-girlfriend, Elaine. Eventually, she believed him when he said it was completely made up.

What she didn't realise was that the song had actually been written by Joe, who secretly penned most of the band's material. He was too shy to let the world know what went on inside his head, and was more than happy to let Ollie take the credit for the songs.

But what neither Ollie nor his girlfriend knew was that *Distant Lovers* had been written about someone in particular. When Ollie stood at the front of the stage, closed his eyes and crooned the words to a gripped audience, he was really singing Joe's feelings of longing out loud. Feelings of longing for the girl he could never have.

Kerry.

Unaware of the confusion of emotions behind it, the captivated crowd listened intently as the final strains of Andy's bass echoed through the room, before roaring their approval.

For the first time that evening Ollie's face broke out into a grin. Now that he had their attention, he knew the rest would be easy.

• • •

"Oh, Ollie, you were brilliant, I'm so proud of you."

Kerry reached up and kissed Ollie gently on the lips. Sliding his hand round her waist he pulled her towards him and they kissed again, though this time it was a lingering, romantic, *proper* kiss that Kerry wanted to go on for ever.

They stood in the dark at Kerry's front gate. It was gone midnight; long after the band had finished their set, she had hung around while the boys cleared up their equipment and talked to Derek and Nick. Matt had taken most of the gear away in his car with a little assistance from Joe, leaving Ollie free to give Kerry a ride home on his treasured Vespa which, for once, was miraculously working.

"It wasn't so bad, was it?" mused Ollie. "Not once we got everyone's attention. I tell you though, at one point I thought we were gonners. We were dying up there; no one was listening."

"I know. I was so angry I wanted to run on stage and grab the microphone to shout at everyone to shut up," Kerry chuckled. "But once you made them listen, the rest was brilliant."

"We could have done with a few more bums on seats," continued Ollie, leaning against the Bellamys' front wall and folding his arms across his chest, "but I suppose it could have been worse. *You* might have been the only one there."

"Was Derek disappointed with the turn-out?"

"Not really. Or at least I don't think so. He never said anything and he didn't cancel our gig next Thursday, so I guess he must have been pretty happy. Did the others say anything to you about what they thought?"

Kerry came up to him and unfolded his arms, placing herself between them and his warm body. "Everyone – even those two Dutch lads – said how amazing you all were," she smiled, looking up at him adoringly. "Except for Cat, who was too busy trying to flog tickets for her pantomime to everyone there."

Ollie laughed. "Well, I can't say I'm surprised. Cat wouldn't be Cat if she didn't try her luck. 'Specially if she spotted people who were worse the wear for beer and easy targets for her."

"It wouldn't have been so bad except that she dragged Maya off too, to help her in her campaign to sell out the performance single-handed," Kerry went on.

"Maya!" Ollie exclaimed. "Somehow I can't imagine her steaming in there as Cat's sidekick. It's not really her style, is it?"

"Well, it didn't get that far. Maya managed to unpeel herself from Cat's clutches and escape back to the rest of us after she'd sold a pair of tickets to Rudi and Marc."

"Which I can't imagine Cat would have found a problem at all, can you?"

Ollie bent down and nuzzled his face into Kerry's neck, and soon they were kissing again.

Finally, Ollie broke away.

"I'd better get going or I'll want to stay like this all night," he said, stroking her hair with one hand and smiling. "Are we still on for this Saturday night?"

"Yeah," Kerry replied. "Sorry it's not going to be very exciting though. Babysitting Lewis isn't the most romantic thing to do on a weekend, is it?"

"It'll be nice," Ollie assured her. "I'll bring a video and a pizza, and we can cuddle up on the sofa."

"Except one whiff of pizza and we'll have Lewis sitting between us on the sofa," laughed Kerry.

"Well, I'll make sure it's a really slushy video," grinned Ollie. "He can't stand those – he'll be running back to bed in no time!"

With that, he kissed her lightly on the nose and walked over to his moped, pulling his helmet on as he went. Turning the key in the ignition he gave her a wave then roared off into the night.

CHAPTER 11

• •

PRINCE CHARMING

Catrina studied herself from every angle in the full-length mirror in her bedroom and announced, "And today, we're happy to welcome as our guest, Catrina Osgood, the famous and talented actress!"

Holding out her hands with palms to the front, Cat muttered "Thank you, thank you!" as she imagined herself taking her seat on *This Morning*.

She looked quite demure in a cream wraparound top, calf-length, A-line, rose-print skirt and little black lace-up boots with humble two-inch heels. Perfect for daytime telly.

Not that she was expecting an invitation on the show *quite* yet.

After being given a couple of days to brush up on her lines, Cat had had an extra rehearsal with

Glenn after college on Friday (he was still pretty frosty, but she was determined to win him over yet), and another full run-through the previous afternoon with the full cast.

Later today, she was spending a couple of hours with Jeff, "polishing the rough edges". Cat wasn't exactly thrilled by the sound of that, but she didn't take offence. She owed her break to Jeff and she was ready to listen to everything he had to say to her.

"Try and get into Cinderella's head a little more," he'd also said to her after yesterday's rehearsal. "I think you need to tone down the exuberance just a touch..."

Cat looked at her reflection again. He was right – she'd yelled her way happily through all the sad songs the day before and even tried to put a tap-dance in at one point. She'd let her excitement take over in the last few days and gone back to her loud and lairy self.

Nope, she'd got the part. She'd proved to Jeff that she could act. So now she had to find her demure side. Wherever that was.

I could picture Mum as the Wicked Stepmother, treating me cruelly and making me do all the chores around the house... she daydreamed herself into her role. *Sonja's one of my Ugly Sisters. Maybe Matt's the other one...*

None of the boys she knew in town fitted the part of Prince Charming; someone kind and thoughtful, who didn't take the mickey out of her or stare at her boobs instead of her face when they talked to her.

Never mind, she thought to herself, humming *Some Day My Prince Will Come* as she left the flat and made her way towards the End.

●　●　●

Only Joe was there, sitting at the usual table by the window, having staked it out amid the steady Sunday morning rush of customers.

She smiled fondly as she saw his earnest face.

He's a real sweetie, our Joey, she thought as she walked over to him. *Kind and thoughtful...*

It suddenly occurred to Cat that her shy mate was about the closest she was going to get to a Prince Charming to practise on.

Yeah, he'll do to help get me into my part, she decided.

She leant over and surprised him with a kiss on the cheek.

"Hello, Joe, it's lovely to see you. How are you?"

Joe was stunned by this blatant show of affection. In all the time he'd known her, Cat had never tried that one on him before. A cutting comment about something or other was her usual opening gambit.

"Er, hello," he blushed. "Um, I'm fine. You?"

"Oh, you know," she said, waving her hand in front of him theatrically, "coping with my insignificant little life. Can I get you something? My treat for my sweet Prince Charming?"

"No thanks."

Joe looked away quickly in the hope that she wouldn't notice he'd gone an even deeper shade of red. Her odd behaviour was making him feel decidedly uncomfortable.

Cat strolled up to the counter where Ollie was serving. As she did so, the door opened and Matt, Gabrielle, Kerry and Sonja walked in.

"Hi, everyone!" chirruped Cat. "Nice to see you. Ooh, Sonja, that coat really suits you; I love it. What can I get you all to drink?"

"If you're thinking of asking to borrow it, forget it," Sonja shot back, eyeing her cousin suspiciously. She didn't think she'd ever heard Cat pay her a compliment about something she was wearing. What was the girl up to now?

Cat pouted girlishly and looked hurt.

"I wouldn't dream of asking you to lend it to me," she replied softly. "I was just trying to be nice, that's all."

Sonja went over to the window seat to sit next to Joe. "I'll have a chocolate mocha if you're buying," she shouted over her shoulder. "That would be 'nice'."

Matt and Kerry put in their orders with Cat and came and sat alongside the others.

"What's with her?" hissed Matt. "Is she having a funny turn or something?"

"She was like it with me, too," Joe whispered back. "Really sweet and totally insincere. I think she's losing her marbles."

"And she looks odd, too," Matt continued. "Hardly recognisable with that girlie hair and make-up. She looks... ill."

"That's what I said the other day," added Sonja. "I still think she's after someone, a guy who's so totally different from her that she's trying to change everything about herself to make him like her."

"She must have it bad if she'll go to those lengths then," Matt replied. "It's not usually Cat's style at all. I'll ask her..."

Cat came back, all smiles.

"Ollie really is lovely, you know," she said, looking at Kerry. "You're so lucky to have a boyfriend like him. He's always so cheerful and pleasant. I think it's great that you two got together. I really do."

Kerry stifled a giggle. It was as if Cat had just read a few lines out of some slushy novel.

Sonja burst out laughing. "OK, come on, Cat," she sniggered. "What sort of game is this? Are you after someone?"

"I don't know what you're talking about," Cat replied, a look of surprise slapped across her face. "I'm only saying what I think. Is that so wrong?"

"No, not at all," said Sonja. "Only when you normally say what you think, it generally involves slagging someone off. So what we're all dying to know is whether this complete turnaround in character has got something to do with a guy?"

Cat fluttered her barely mascara'd eyelashes in shock. "No it's not! Isn't a girl allowed to be pleasant without everyone getting suspicious?"

She was quite enjoying this red herring that her friends had chosen to believe. It would keep them off the trail about what she was really up to, and their shock when the curtain came up on the stage would be even better.

"Not when that girl happens to be you," chuckled Matt. "You're after one of the Dutch lads, aren't you. Think this new act will have them falling at your feet?"

"You mean Marc and Rudi?" she said wide-eyed. "Oh, no, I was just being friendly to them. Lovely guys though. I'd invite them to a couple of parties, but I don't think I'll be able to go now…"

"Why ever not?" Kerry asked. "It's not like you to miss out on a party."

"Well, I expect I'll have chores to do around the flat. Mum keeps saying I don't do enough at home; I expect she'll want to keep me in over Christmas to help her out."

Cat paused for effect. "I don't mind of course," she added, "I mean, Mum works so hard in the office all day, then she comes home and has to cook and clean, it's no wonder she's tired and grouchy a lot of the time. I've always said she takes on too much. If I can help her out in any way, then I will."

She looked from one friend to the next; each face her eyes fell on looked more startled than the last.

Ollie walked over with a tray of drinks for everyone.

"Oh, Ollie, how sweet of you to bring them over," Cat cooed. "You should have called me – I would have come and fetched them. I know how busy you are."

Ollie looked at Cat aghast.

"Huh?" he said, half smiling as though trying to get the joke.

The others sniggered, amused by his reaction.

"It's OK, Ol," said Matt. "Cat's trying to con

us into thinking she's got a conscience. But don't worry, she'll soon be back to her old ways."

Still flummoxed by what was going on around him, Ollie placed the tray of drinks on the table and wandered off back behind the serving counter. He suddenly felt safer there.

• • •

Anna glanced around the café. It was busy, buzzing with music from the jukebox and lots of Sunday morning chatter, but no one needed serving.

She scrabbled for a few silver coins from her jeans pocket and went over to the pay phone on the wall. Dialling her brother's number, she crossed her fingers that he would be in so that she could finally sort out when he was coming and how he was planning to let their mother know about his change of plans.

When Owen picked up the phone, Anna jumped in.

"Thank God you're back," she said irritably. "I've been desperate to get you for days."

"Hey, what's up?" Owen said, concerned. "Is something wrong?"

Realising that the urgency in her voice must be worrying him, Anna calmed herself.

"No, no, not at all. Well, nothing major. It's just that I've been on the phone to Mum and she thinks you're going to stay with her for Christmas. Haven't you told her?"

"Told her what?" Owen asked.

"That you're coming to Winstead instead."

There was an prolonged silence at the other end of the line before Owen spoke.

"But I *am* going to Mum's. I've already told you that, Anna."

"Huh?" Anna was lost in confusion.

She glanced back in the direction of the crowd sitting in the window seat and saw Sonja laughing and joking with the others.

"Hang on, Owen," she spoke more quietly into the receiver, "I spoke to Sonja the other day and she said you'd changed your mind and that you were coming here instead."

"Uhh... so *that's* why she sounded so cool when I was trying to explain that I was going home for Christmas the other night," Owen sighed. "I thought her reaction was a bit odd."

"But how could she get it so wrong?" whispered Anna. Her own disappointment felt like a lead weight in her stomach. Sonja's disappointment when she told her was only going to make it worse...

"I don't know," said Owen, with a tinge of

annoyance in his voice. "It was late, I was sleepy; I probably didn't explain myself very well. And then Sonja's sister Lottie kept butting in on the other extension."

"Oh, listen, it's OK," Anna tried to reassure him. "It's just one of those things. It's no big deal..."

Owen wasn't coming. Anna was going to be on her own after all.

It was a big deal.

CHAPTER 12

• •

OH NO HE'S NOT. DEFINITELY

"There's *definitely* a guy involved."

"I can't imagine Cat changing herself for a bloke, she's far too pig-headed."

"Maybe she's got in with some strange cult."

"You don't think it could be that she's genuinely trying to become a nicer person, do you?"

"No way!"

Once Cat had left the café to go and meet up with Jeff at the college, the others carried on trying to analyse her bizarre behaviour. They had been joined by Maya, with the occasional contribution from Ollie and Anna as they continued to serve the constant stream of customers passing through.

"If it *is* a guy, it must be pretty serious for her to be making such an effort to impress him,"

Maya said, "but I wonder why she's not letting on who he is. Cat's not usually shy about admitting who she fancies."

"Unless she's embarrassed by him," Sonja replied. "He might be a complete nerd or a train-spotter or a religious nut or something."

"Or all three," chuckled Matt. "Or maybe she's fallen for the lad that's playing Prince Charming in that panto she's doing."

"She called *me* her sweet Prince Charming earlier on," Joe blurted out.

"Well, that's it then. It's *you* she's after, Joe!" roared Matt, slapping his hand against his thigh at the ludicrousness of the thought. "Aren't you the lucky guy?"

Everyone sniggered, and not for the first time that day Joe turned crimson and wished he'd kept his mouth shut. The very idea of Cat fancying someone like him was ridiculous.

Wasn't it?

"Anyway, I'm bored with talking about Cat," Matt carried on. "I was thinking of throwing a party at my place on Friday, to make it up to Gaby for dragging her along to my old man's do at the golf club. What d'you say?"

"Oh, yes!" Sonja gasped, her eyes goggling at Gabrielle. "I'd forgotten you were going there last night. How was it? Did you have a *groovy* time?"

"Er, not exactly," said Gabrielle quietly. "Let's just say it's a once in a lifetime experience I don't want to repeat. I think me and Matt were the only non-geriatrics there."

"Sounds grim," Sonja laughed. "You must really love him to allow him to take you to such a cruddy do like that."

Gabrielle smiled and looked shyly down at her hands resting on the table top.

"Cheers, Son," said Matt. "Thanks for rubbing it in. So, about this party..."

"He said, changing the subject," Sonja grinned. "I think it's a great idea, a chance to get into the Christmas spirit. I don't suppose Owen will be down by then, will he, Anna? But I guess I could drag myself along to help you out with the numbers. Hey, Anna, thought any more about this welcome party idea?"

"Er – speak to you about that later," said Anna, glad to see a new batch of customers walk in and need serving.

● ● ●

The next half hour was so busy that Anna was only dimly aware of her friends saying their farewells as they drifted off one by one.

It was only when she caught her breath finally

that she saw Sonja sitting alone in the window booth.

It's now or never, Anna told herself, striding over.

"You haven't heard from Owen then?" Sonja asked, voicing the only thing on her mind.

"Actually, Sonja, I have. I spoke to him a little while ago."

"When?"

"Earlier," Anna replied vaguely, but found herself half-heartedly nodding in the direction of the phone on the wall.

"*That* was Owen you were talking to?" said Sonja incredulously. "But why didn't you call me over? Didn't he want to speak to me?"

Anna could tell she was alarming Sonja more than helping her now. She was obviously jumping to conclusions; panicking that Owen's lack of contact had more ominous implications.

"Don't worry," she said soothingly. "He's been on a course for work this week, which is why he hasn't been in touch."

Sonja didn't look reassured. "And?"

"I wanted to tell you what he said when it got quieter," Anna tried to explain. "Listen, Son, he's *not* coming for Christmas."

Sonja looked shocked. "What?"

"It's all my fault for trying to persuade him to

come in the first place. If I hadn't suggested it, then you two wouldn't have been speaking about it, and you wouldn't have got this all muddled," Anna sighed.

"But he said he *was* coming..." Sonja almost whimpered.

Anna felt like doing the same. It was all right for Sonja – she still had a family to spend Christmas Day with. Anna had no one.

"Owen was never planning on coming here for Christmas. He thinks you must have been talking at cross purposes when you spoke the other night. I'm really sorry, Son. I'm sure he'll speak to you himself to explain."

"Oh."

Anna could see the disappointment on Sonja's face as well as hear it in her voice.

"Oh, well," Sonja continued, smiling weakly, "I guess we'll just have to party on without him. I take it he's going to your Mum's after all?"

Anna nodded.

Sonja looked away. She was heartbroken. She'd been so looking forward to this Christmas, imagining all sorts of romantic scenarios involving her and Owen, and now she didn't feel like celebrating at all.

But then a glimmer of an idea came to her...

"*I* know, Anna," she said, her face brightening.

"Why don't you invite Owen and your mum down to spend Christmas with you? That way you get to see them both, and I get to see Owen!"

It was the worst suggestion Anna had ever heard. There was no way she'd invite her mum down, although Sonja wasn't to know that. None of the gang knew the ins and outs of Anna's past problems, and Sonja came from such a close-knit family herself, no wonder she thought she'd had a brilliant idea.

"Er, no, that won't work. For one thing, I don't have the space to put Owen and Mum up," Anna tried to explain.

"That's OK," Sonja cut in excitedly. "There's that sweet little B&B along the road from me..."

"Sonja, my mum can't afford train travel and B&Bs just like that, and I don't have the money to—"

"But Owen could treat her, now he's got this job!" persisted Sonja.

"*No*, Sonja," Anna objected, a determined tone in her voice.

Sonja looked at her in surprise. She'd never seen Anna riled.

"It's not just that. To be honest, Mum and I don't get along too well. We're OK, you know, we get by, but spending Christmas together just isn't going to happen."

"Oh, right, I didn't realise," Sonja replied, confused but unwilling to pry. "I mean, I know you don't go home for visits…"

Anna stared out the window as Sonja's words fizzled out awkwardly. Her last memory of her old home was when her mother had told her that they couldn't live under the same roof together.

Yes, so now – thanks to Owen – they were talking again. But she could never truly forgive her mother for the terrible way she'd reacted to the news that her daughter was pregnant, and the even more terrible way she'd reacted when Anna told her she'd decided to have an abortion. At the time when she'd been at her lowest and had needed understanding most, her mum had turned round and given her the opposite.

"You must be disappointed too, Anna, at the way things have turned out," Sonja tried to say comfortingly, without realising just how true her words were.

CHAPTER 13

● ●

A CHANGE OF HEART

Joe sat at a Burger King window seat and tried to sort his head out. He'd recently come to the conclusion that he was quite content with his lot (getting on pretty well with his father in his new life just outside Winstead, which was a bit of a novelty), and felt he had masses to look forward to (a band that seemed to be going somewhere, also a novelty). The only blip was – as always – Kerry.

Maybe, just maybe, he'd started to think, he should try and wean himself off her for good. Loving her in secret was just eating him up inside and made him feel guilty every time he saw Ollie and her together.

How could he be so jealous of his best friend, who trusted him completely?

It wasn't a healthy situation, whichever way you looked at it.

And if I could just get over her, then maybe I could meet someone else, he daydreamed as his uneaten fries went cold. Maybe then the pieces in Joe's jigsaw would fit together. Maybe then he would be truly happy.

Surprisingly, recent events with Cat had forced the issue of Joe's new determination to forget about Kerry. He knew Matt was only joking the other day in the End when he'd suggested she fancied Joe, but it had started him thinking.

Other girls might actually fancy him (not Cat, of course, he was sure) and he would never notice, being too wrapped up in thoughts of the one girl he couldn't have.

Joe wasn't sure what Cat had been up to that day when she'd almost been flirting with him, but he knew he liked the feeling. He wanted to be flirted with, instead of pining in his room, writing meaningful lyrics for someone who was oblivious to how he felt. Being flirted with felt good.

Joe didn't notice the figure walking past the window staring in at him. He didn't see Cat until she was standing in front of him.

"Boo!" she exclaimed, her eyes popping in an exaggerated fashion.

Joe's head shot up. When he realised who it

was, and that he'd just been thinking about her, Joe blushed as though he'd been caught red-handed doing something he shouldn't.

She looks really good, he thought, which made him turn even redder. Joe had always thought Cat wore too much make-up; sometimes he thought she almost looked like a drag queen, she caked it on so thick. But since she'd been toning the look down, he was conscious of the fact that she looked really very pretty. These days you could actually see that she had good skin, and when her lips weren't laden down with lashings of lip gloss, you could make out their true shape.

Even her hair looked better. Ever since Joe had known Catrina, she had been bleaching it, dyeing it, curling it or crucifying it in some way or another. But this latest colour and style were a definite improvement. The cut suited her and the blonde colour was nice and subtle, for a change. She looked much more like 'the girl next door' than Joe could ever remember. He was definitely beginning to see her in a new light...

"You, um, want to hang around, Cat?" he asked. "I was going to get another Coke. You want one?"

"Oh, thanks, Joe," she wrinkled her nose at him. "I'll have an orange juice please."

Joe slid out of the plastic chair and walked over to the counter. As his order was fed into the computer, Joe couldn't help but look back over his shoulder at Cat. She was sitting humming a song to herself as she played with the salt and pepper sachets on the table.

She looks really cute, Joe couldn't help thinking.

When he got back to the table, Cat beamed at him.

"Thanks, Joe," she said. "So tell me, how's my favourite drummer?"

"Um, good," he nodded, unsure of what to say next.

"So what are you and Ollie planning next for The Loud? You're not going to stay playing at that grotty pub for ever, are you?"

It was just the subject to set Joe off. Although he often found it hard talking to girls (even his female friends when they were just one-to-one), get him on his favourite topic of music and he was away. At one point he could have sworn he saw Cat stifle a yawn, but she still seemed to be smiling encouragingly at him, so he carried on.

"I'm sorry, Joe," she interrupted him at one point, "but I've got to go. I've got to go and see someone about a new dress. I'd love to stay here and hear all about the band, but I just can't."

She got up to go. Joe watched her pull layers of outdoor clothes on; then wave goodbye as she strolled out of the door.

With a faraway look in his eyes, he continued staring at the doorway long after she'd gone.

• • •

"How's it going with Prince Charming and the other morons?" asked Vikki, stepping into the pink, frothy gown that one of the two costume designers was holding out for her.

"Thawing out *very*, very slowly," Cat replied, as she stepped into her own costume during this final costume fitting.

"Well, there's no doubting that you and me are the stars of this show, girl, and don't you forget it!" Vikki boomed out confidently.

"Too right – we're the best!" laughed Cat.

The two girls looked at each other, and – reading each other's thoughts – immediately broke out into the chorus of *Simply The Best*, complete with Tina Turner rock chick moves.

"Oi, you two – watch the costumes!" said one of the two girls who were struggling to zip Vikki and Cat up.

The girls broke into giggles, but as soon as they caught sight of each other in the full-length mirror in front of them, their laughter faded away.

"Wow..." muttered Vikki, as she gazed at the vision that was Cat.

"Wow yourself!" Cat managed to mumble back, when the shock of just how amazing she looked finally sank in, and she had a chance to take in Vikki's outfit.

They stood side by side: Cat, pale, blonde and elegant (for once) in a glittering, white, floor-sweeping ballgown and elbow-length white satin gloves; Vikki, dark skin contrasting amazingly with her wildly ornate pink Fairy Godmother dress.

The two girls grinned once again and Vikki held up her hand to her fellow star.

"The best!" they both yelled, as Cat slapped Vikki's hand with her own.

CHAPTER 14

●●●●●●●●●●●●●●●●●●●●●●●●●●●●●

PUTTING ON A BRAVE FACE

"Come on, Anna, sit down for five minutes. You look whacked."

Ollie patted the seat beside her and smiled sympathetically as a grateful Anna slid into it. It was ten to nine on Wednesday night, and the only people left in the café were Anna, who was finishing her shift, and Ollie and Kerry, who had been discussing their family arrangements for Christmas and the New Year.

"You're not wrong," she said, rubbing the back of her neck with one hand. "I'm absolutely bushed. I don't know how you've managed with your shifts here and helping out at the pub."

"I've got this slot in my back – didn't you know?" grinned Ollie. "I just stick industrial-strength batteries in there..."

"God, I could do with a couple of those," Anna smiled. "Look, if you want me to take on a couple of your shifts here to give you a break in the day, I'm more than happy to. Honestly, it's not a problem."

"Thanks, Anna, that's really good of you, I'll bear it in mind," said Ollie, peeling off his apron and dumping it on the table. " So, I meant to ask – what are you doing for Christmas now that Owen isn't coming?"

The bad news about Owen was common knowledge among the gang by now and Ollie had been meaning to broach the subject with Anna as soon as he got a chance. He was worried that she'd be sitting all alone in her flat with not even a cracker for company.

"Uh, at the moment, I guess I'm at a loose end again," Anna answered simply.

"Anna, that's awful," wailed Kerry. "You mean you're going to be stuck in your flat on Christmas Day on your own?"

"Uh, well, when you put it like that it sounds pretty grim, but honestly..." she said, knowing she wasn't about to be honest "...I'm looking forward to just putting my feet up and relaxing. I'll spoil myself with some nice nosh from M&S and veg out in front of the telly. And I'll have no one to argue with over which corny film to watch.

Hey! I'm liking this idea more all the time..."

She thought she was doing a pretty good job of making light of the situation. Especially when the reality was that she wanted to cry. But as Anna looked smilingly from Ollie to Kerry and back again, from the looks on their faces, they were both pretty horrified by the idea.

"Anna, you can't be serious," Ollie protested. "Is that how you want to spend Christmas? In all honesty?"

Anna mulled over the question before replying.

"Well, I'd rather be on a Caribbean cruise," she tried to joke, "but I don't think I can afford it on the wages Nick pays me, do you?"

"Well, you can come and have Christmas lunch with me and my family," Ollie offered. "It's always a laugh."

"I couldn't do that!" Anna said, gobsmacked. "It would be like imposing on your parents!"

"Don't be silly! You can be my token sister. Natasha's spending the holidays over in the States with some rich new mate of hers she met while she was working out there."

"Ollie, I'd feel too uncomfortable, honestly. But thanks."

"Well, at least pop into The Swan at some point. There's usually a great atmosphere – loads of people there, Kerry and Joe'll drop in, maybe a few of the others. It'll be great. I guarantee you'll enjoy it."

"Oh, I'm not sure..." Anna replied. "I'd feel like I was just hanging about and getting in the way."

"Anna, it's a *pub*," cried Ollie, laughing. "How can you *possibly* get in the way? We'll be open till the middle of the afternoon. So believe me, if you're in the way then so will the hundred or so other people who come in on Christmas Day!"

"Ollie's right," Kerry said, keen to back up her boyfriend. She hated the idea of Anna spending the day on her own. Kerry couldn't imagine anything sadder.

"You'll have a great time. I'll definitely pop by, if only to chuck Ollie his present. And I bet there'll be quite a few people there you'll know. Surely it beats being stuck in your flat on your own *all* day."

Again Anna felt a lump in her throat, as if tears were not far away. It was good to have friends.

• • •

Sonja too was trying to get over her disappointment over Owen's no-show. If there was to be no romance and no welcome surprise party, she was just going to have to be brave. She should come up with another way of filling her time, making sure she didn't have a second to mope.

The band would be playing as usual later tonight, Matt's party was tomorrow and Cat's pantomime on Saturday; but she needed more than that lot to keep her longing for Owen at bay. Sonia willed her brain to come up with something.

Maya and Joe had already beaten Kerry and herself round to the End after college, and Matt was sitting with his arm wrapped protectively around Gabrielle, guarding her like a prized work of art.

"You know, we all ought to meet up somewhere again on Christmas Eve, like we did last year," Sonja said brightly, sliding into the booth. "We could go to Enigma – they're supposed to be putting on a brilliant night."

"Sounds good," replied Matt, "especially since I know the DJ who's doing it, so I might be able to wangle a few free tickets for us."

"I don't know. I got turned away for being under age last time we went!" winced Maya.

"Don't worry," Matt reassured her. "If we get passes off the DJ, then we can just sail in, no problem."

"I know – we could all have a kissing competition, like last year too!" Sonja beamed. "See how many snogs you can get in say, an hour.

I'm bound to win, now that you're off the scene, Matt."

"Oh, I dunno," Gabrielle piped up, "if the first prize is good enough, I might give you lot a run for your money myself!"

Matt looked at his girlfriend as though she'd just smacked him in the teeth. He never expected her to come out with something like that.

"It's OK," she smiled, patting him on the leg, "I'm only joking."

Matt gave her a squeeze and rested his head on top of hers. He felt so lucky to have met someone like Gabrielle. He wouldn't miss the snogging competition at all, not with her around.

He was convinced this was going to be his best Christmas ever. He had been buying Gabrielle presents for weeks and had spent loads of money. He wanted to make her Christmas as special as he possibly could, because as far as he was concerned, she was worth it.

"Show of hands for Enigma then!" trilled Sonja, counting their unanimous approval.

Though Sonja would have swapped all the clubs in the world for a romantic night in with Owen this Christmas Eve.

CHAPTER 15

● ●

ON A HIGH

"Coo-ey! Joe! Wait up!"

Joe was wandering along the road, on his way to Matt's house to help him set up for the party. He had been mulling over The Loud's gig last night as he walked, inwardly congratulating himself when he'd played well, working out why he'd gone wrong when he hadn't.

Overall, it was a better show than the one the week before. Everyone felt that. For one, there were more people in the audience, and instead of the band having to fight for them to take notice, people seemed to be listening from the opening song onwards. It was good, he told himself, really good.

He turned to see who was calling him.

It was Cat. Again.

Joe felt he'd hardly been out of her sight these past few days. It was as if she was following him around. Mind you, he couldn't help but be pleased to see her. Especially since she was being so pleasant to him at the moment.

"Hello, Cat," he grinned. "Long time no see."

"Hello, my handsome Prince Charming," she said, lowering her eyes and fluttering her eyelashes at him. "You know we must stop meeting like this. People will start to talk."

She linked her arm through his as they strolled up the road.

"Looking forward to Matt's party?" he asked her almost nervously.

Cat wrinkled her nose. "I'm not going."

Joe was alarmed to realise he felt disappointed. "Why not?"

"Well, I might come later, if I'm not too tired. It's just that I'm on my way to college – it's the first showing of Cinderella tonight."

"Tonight? But I thought there was just one show – the one we're all coming to tomorrow..." Joe was amazed that Cat hadn't mentioned this to anyone before.

"Yeah, tonight is for all the kids. You know – the ones from the charity the proceeds go to."

"Right," nodded Joe. "So – how are you feeling about it?"

"Jittery," she laughed with a wobbly voice. "It's just that feeling that I'm bound to fluff my lines..."

It was the most candid Cat had been so far about the pantomime. Somehow, she didn't mind telling Joe more than she would the others. She felt that he would be one of the few people not to laugh if she fell flat on her face.

"Wow, you mean you've got lines to say as well? I didn't realise. I thought you were just in the chorus."

"Well... I do have one or two things to say... But, actually, I'm convinced that the less you have to say, the bigger a thing it becomes in your head."

"Don't worry, Cat," Joe reassured her, "I'm sure you'll knock 'em dead."

"Do you think so?" said Cat, genuinely pleased. "That's such a lovely thing to say, Joe. I hope you're right."

"I'm sure I am," he replied, smiling at her. "I'm really looking forward to seeing you up there on stage tomorrow. You're going to be brilliant."

"Oh, Joe, I could kiss you," Cat said. "In fact..."

She stopped in the street, reached up to Joe's face and planted a soft kiss on his cheek. Joe blushed furiously as he felt a little tingle of excitement run through his body.

Wow! he thought.

Cat giggled at his reaction.

"You're such a sweet boy, Joe," she cooed. "Why haven't you got a girlfriend?"

Joe blushed purple. He didn't quite know how to answer that one.

"I... er... uh..." he spluttered, looking for suitable words. All he could think of was: *because I'm a dork... because I'm so weird-looking no girl could possibly be interested in me... because I have no confidence in myself and therefore can't chat girls up.*

Fortunately, he stopped himself from saying any of those things; instead he looked at the ground and wished it would swallow him up.

"*I* know why it is," Cat announced.

Oh, God, what's she going to say? he wondered desperately. *Please don't be a bitch, Catrina. I couldn't stand it if you said something horrible.*

"It's because you're too nice," smiled Cat, snuggling further into his arm. "And you're kind and unassuming. And all the girls in Winstead don't realise what they're missing out on by not dating you. That's why."

Joe's mouth dropped open in amazement. No one had ever said anything so flattering about him before in his life, not even his mum. Certainly not a girl of his own age.

He looked incredulously at Cat as they walked along together, half expecting to see her smirk, then shout out something like "Hah! Only joking, you loser!" But she didn't. She was staring off into the distance somewhere, completely unaware of the effect her words were having on him.

He was at a loss as to what to say next, so they walked on in silence for a while.

"Right, this is where I must leave you," Cat suddenly announced as they came to a turning not far from Matt's. "Much as I'd like to stay cuddling you, Joe, poor little ole me has work to do. So..."

She unpeeled herself from his protecting arm and gave him a girlish smile "...I hope you have a good time tonight. And I hope I can count on you to be there to support me tomorrow."

"Oh, yes! Of course I'll be there," Joe grinned, a tender look coming over his face. "I'll be right there in the front row cheering you on."

"Thanks, Prince Charming, I appreciate it."

Once again Cat planted a kiss on her escort's cheek. Then she turned and went off down the main road.

Joe made the rest of his way round to Matt's floating on a fluffy cloud, high above the ground.

• • •

The party-goers were out in force at Matt's that night. It seemed as though half of St Mark's sixth form was there, plus a smattering of Gabrielle's friends and loads of Matt's mates he'd got to know through DJing.

Although it was bitterly cold outside, Matt (with Joe's help) had built a bonfire in the garden, and that was where most people seemed to have congregated. Frenetic dance sounds blared out from Matt's speakers and people kept themselves warm by dancing round the brightly flickering blaze.

Joe spotted the others hovering beside the conservatory door, far enough away from the speakers and the dancers to be able to talk without having to shout or dodge the odd flailing arm or two.

Joe was on such a high after his encounter with Cat, he bounded up to Ollie and leapt on to his back.

"Hiya, mate!" he hollered. "Happy Christmas!"

Ollie collapsed to the ground and soon the two boys were rolling about on the grass, play fighting like a couple of eight-year-olds. The rest of the friends stood around and egged them on, only shouting warnings when they got a little too close to the bonfire. By the time Joe and Ollie stood up, they were so covered in dirt they looked like they'd been mud-wrestling.

"We were good last night, weren't we, Joe?" Ollie beamed at his friend.

"Brilliant, mate! The best. Where's Billy and Andy – are they coming tonight?"

"Oh, they're around somewhere. We should've got them to bring their instruments; we could have played a gig right here on Matt's lawn."

"Nah, not without charging people to see us!" grinned Joe. "We shouldn't have to do freebies for anyone any more, not now we're rock'n'roll stars!"

"Ooh, *you're* cocky!" Sonja laughed. "I don't think I've ever heard you sounding so confident, Joe. Your head will be getting too big for its own good if you carry on like that."

Joe grinned impishly. He really did feel very good about himself right now; his confidence had suddenly grown to mammoth proportions.

"Aw, I think it's great," Kerry said. "You lot were so excellent last night, I'm not surprised you're still on a high."

No one realised that last night's gig wasn't the only reason for Joe's sudden high spirits. He only wished Cat could be there to share it with him.

"You'll have record companies fighting to sign you up soon," added Maya. "Just so long as you remember who your friends were when you're on *Top of the Pops*."

"Nah," Ollie smirked. "We'll be too busy fighting off the groupies to bother with you guys then."

Kerry went to slap Ollie on the head. He ducked and instead she caught Joe on the cheek.

"Oh, Joe, I'm sorry!" cried Kerry as he reeled away from her in shock.

The startled look on his face, and the horror on Kerry's, soon had everyone in fits of laughter – it looked like a scene from an old black and white Laurel and Hardy sketch.

"Just think, Kez, in years to come, your claim to fame will be that you slapped Joe Gladwin around the face," Sonja chuckled. "It'll be the equivalent of saying you did it to Liam Gallagher or Jay Kay."

Joe looked confused.

"But they don't play drums," he said.

"Joe!" Sonja shot back, exasperated, "I realise that – you know what I mean!"

"Oh." Joe shrugged and began giggling again. Normally, he would have been embarrassed to show himself up like that. But not tonight.

Tonight nothing could touch him.

"I'm freezing," Maya suddenly whimpered, shivering in the cold night air.

"Come on, Maya, I'll soon warm you up." Joe grabbed her by the hand and dragged her into the body of dancers and began dancing wildly, still holding her hand.

"You're in a good mood," she laughed as he twirled her round and round to the music.

"I am," he grinned back. "I'm in a *blinding* mood. Never felt better in my life."

Joe's whole face was lit up.

"Oh, yeah?" Maya said knowingly. "What's her name?"

You'll never guess, he wanted to shout. *It's Cat!*

He didn't, of course. He just carried on dancing, smirking to himself. Joe was used to keeping secrets and this was one he was definitely going to keep to himself...

CHAPTER 16

• •

CAT'S BIG NIGHT

Cat spent most of Saturday in a state of heightened stress. This method acting lark was beginning to get to her. It wouldn't be so bad if the character she was playing was a bit spunky, someone go-getting and gutsy. But Cinderella? To be honest, Cat was heartily sick of the pathetic little wretch. Once tonight was over, she would be glad to get back to being herself again.

Cat figured it might have something to do with the fact that her mother had been nauseatingly nice to her all week; had even asked if she should come and see this 'little play' of her daughter's. Cat had quickly put her off. The last thing she wanted was to be aware of her mother's presence in the audience: she wasn't really up for the criticism she was bound to get at the end of it.

Of course, Sylvia Osgood's temporary niceness (and it had to be temporary: Cat's mum didn't usually waste much time on pleasantries) had to be caused by Cat's new-found enthusiasm for housework (also temporary). However, Cat now had to grudgingly admit to herself that she actually preferred it when they were at each other's throats – the sniping was much more bearable than having her mother clucking and gushing about how wonderful it was to come home to a spotless flat.

That was something else she'd have to rectify once this performance was over...

As she sat on the edge of her bed reading through her stage directions one last time, an awful thought struck Cat.

What if it's a disaster tonight? she fretted, even though the night before – with an audience of thrilled kids – had gone brilliantly. *What if I do something stupid, when my friends are in the audience?*

Cat pushed the notion to the back of her head; it really didn't bear thinking about.

Anyway, the solution was simple, if dramatic.

If I'm awful tonight, I'll just have to leave home and never come back....

● ● ●

Joe started queuing outside the drama hall of Winstead College at 6.30 pm, half an hour before the doors opened and an hour before the show started. He was the first person there.

That didn't bother Joe: he'd promised Cat that he and the others would be in the front row cheering her on, and that's exactly where he intended to be. Everyone had already bought their tickets from Cat and now all he had to do was go in and bagsy a bunch of seats.

As he stood jumping up and down on the spot in a desperate (though largely futile) effort to keep warm, he consoled himself with the fact that he was sure Cat would appreciate the support. He thought of her looking at him all dewy-eyed and calling him her Prince Charming again and felt a warm shiver shoot up his spine.

Maya was the next to show up, five minutes before the doors opened.

"Hi, Joe," she said when she saw him shivering at the head of the queue. "Crikey, you're keen, aren't you? How long have you been here?"

"Oh, not long," Joe lied. "Just wanted to be sure to get those front seats."

"You must either be a big panto fan or keen to see what kind of performance Cat puts on!"

Joe smiled. He wondered whether to say anything to Maya about Cat. He knew she could be trusted to keep her mouth shut, and he did feel like shouting his feelings from the rooftops... and yet something stopped him.

Maybe it was the knowledge that Maya was already the only person in the world who knew about his feelings for Kerry. Maybe she would find it difficult to believe that Joe could fall for two girls at once.

Or maybe it was because Joe himself wasn't sure what he felt for the normally man-eating Cat. His emotions were certainly strong, but at the same time very different from those he still felt for Kerry.

"Actually, I can't wait to see Cat," he admitted, "I think she'll be great, don't you?"

"Yeah, I've got no doubts on that score," laughed Maya. "I mean, Cat loves an audience; add that to the fact that she's one big drama queen and I think you've got the perfect ingredients for a great career in panto. I'm sure she'll make her presence felt, even at the back of a crowd scene. She'll manage to get herself noticed somehow or other."

Joe chuckled. "It's funny how much she's changed, isn't it? She looks heaps better now she's got rid of all that make-up."

"I know," Maya agreed. "I didn't realise until recently that she had skin under all that foundation. She's actually really pretty in the flesh, so to speak."

"I think she's gorgeous," said Joe without thinking. Then realising he was being a bit too open, he checked himself by spluttering, "Erm, you know, if you like that sort of thing."

Maya eyed her friend.

I wonder if you've got a crush on Cat, she thought. *God help you if you do!*

• • •

It was five minutes to curtain up. Cat peered from out from behind a chink in the safety curtain to take her first glimpse of the audience beyond. She wanted to see what was going on out there before the lights went down, after which she knew she would only be able to see the first couple of rows.

The place was packed. Cat's heart started beating even more wildly than before. A thrill of excitement shot through her body at the sight of all those people who'd come to see her.

She scoured the audience to see if there was anyone she recognised. There were a few familiar faces from Winstead College, plus a smattering of girls she'd got to know on the beauty therapy course.

She suddenly spied Matt and Gabrielle walking

down the centre aisle towards the front. As they got to the first row and made their way to the middle, right in front of the stage, Cat's heart missed a beat. Then she spotted Joe and the others all along that row, frighteningly close to where she would be performing up on the stage.

My God! I didn't realise they'd be so near – the kids last night seemed a lot further away... she gulped.

Cat felt the nerves she'd so far managed to control engulf her and her stomach began to tighten until she could hardly breathe. They were so close that she could even make out the writing on the cover of the programme Joe was scrutinising. In fact, she could also make out the shocked expression on Joe's face as he turned to a particular page...

"Come on, Cat," said Jeff, pulling her away from the curtain. "We're about to start..."

CHAPTER 17

● ●

...HAPPILY EVER AFTER

Cat took up her position on-stage and waited for the opening bars of the music to begin. She watched nervously as she saw the lights dim beyond the safety curtain and a hush suddenly come over the audience. Expectation hung in the air, weighing heavily on Cat's shoulders.

She looked around at the other members of the cast standing at their positions for this opening scene. They looked how she felt – deathly white, tense, anxious.

Those weren't kids out there tonight; this was an audience of friends, family and paying members of the public. And somehow that made it much harder.

Cat tried to recall her opening line.

It was gone.

Her mind was a blank sheet of paper. She felt the panic rise from her stomach to the dryness of her mouth. She was holding a besom broom with which she was supposed to sweep the floor, but her body was so tense she could feel the knuckles of her hands throbbing with pain where Cat was hanging on to it so tightly.

She was aware that the curtain was being raised and blinked into the bright lights from beyond the stage, jumping as she heard the first strains of music booming through the speakers. Then she was aware of the audience clapping as they saw the actors up there on the stage.

Squinting out into the audience Cat saw all her friends in the front once again; Joe gazing dumbstruck from the cast list page of the programme where her picture was beside the title role, up to Cinderella in all her ragged glory in front of him.

And beside him, she could see Sonja mouthing the words, "Oh, my God!"

From the corner of her eye she could see a glimmer of pink in the wings and knew without looking that Vikki was there, willing her to do well.

"Way to go, Cat!" Matt's distinctive holler rose above the music.

Suddenly, Cat felt a surge of pride rush through her body. Her nerves dissolved into nothing, her opening lines rushed back into her head and, as the noise died down, she began to play her part.

As if by magic, Catrina Osgood *was* Cinderella.

• • •

"She's really good, isn't she?" Sonja whispered to Kerry half-way through the first act.

"Absolutely fantastic," Kerry murmured back. "I can't believe she's got the lead part."

"I know – shocker. I don't know how she managed to keep it to herself. Very un-Catlike."

"But then Cat hasn't been herself recently, has she? Have you noticed that the act she's putting on up there is the same one she's been putting on in front of us for the last week or so?"

"Uh-huh. Kind of all falls into place now, doesn't it?"

"Yeah. I wonder if she'll get back to being her usual catty self once this is over."

"God, I hope so."

The girls looked at each other and giggled.

Someone else who recognised the demure little girl up there on stage was Joe. He sat transfixed by Cat's performance, a mixture of admiration and shock running through his mind as he watched her.

Joe wasn't stupid; like the girls, he had soon

worked out where Cat's performance had come from. All that doe-eyed "you're such a sweetie!" stuff she'd turned on him – it was all a charade to help her get into the part.

As the truth hit him, his heart sank. How could he have been so dumb to be taken in by the little-girl-lost act? And to think that he had almost convinced himself he fancied her. It was, well... it was a joke. He was a joke.

Cat's going to turn right back into Cat at the stroke of midnight, he thought to himself, then started to shake with suppressed laughter at the very idea (much to the surprise of Sonja and Anna who were sitting on either side of him).

● ● ●

"There – *told* you there was a lad involved..."

Joe gazed in the direction that Sonja was pointing.

He, Sonja and the others were pushing through the crowds of well-wishers in the corridor that let to the back-stage area. Each member of the cast – still in their costumes – seemed to have their own fan club gathered around them, chattering and congratulating them.

Up ahead, Joe could see Cinderella in her glittery white ballgown, leaning coquettishly back against the wall. He noticed that the boy who'd played Prince Charming was staring deep into her eyes, looking as smitten as his character had under the spotlights not so long ago.

It looked to Joe as if she'd been working that old black Cat magic again.

"Hi, guys!" Cat yelped as she saw them, waving at them with a hand that held a very un-fairytale princess accessory. A cigarette.

Ollie flapped his hand to get rid of the cloud of smoke before kissing Cat on the cheek.

"Well done, you secretive old boot!" he laughed.

Cat gave a typical, dirty Cat-cackle and turned to her other friends with a swish of floor-sweeping fabric. Prince Charming seemed to be hovering, unsure whether he was dismissed or not.

Hesitating for a second, Cat turned and gave Glenn a cheeky wink. "Catch you later at the cast party, babe!"

"Congratulations, Cat!" Anna grabbed her attention, giving her a hug. "You were fantastic! You must be really pleased."

"Oh I am, Anna," Cat gushed, "I'm absolutely delighted. Jeff the director's already talking about what show we should do next year and what part I should play!"

As well as the cigarette, the lecherous look at her co-star and the throaty laugh, Joe noticed another true Cat-ism had crept back already... a rich red slash of lipstick. She'd obviously slapped it on the minute the curtain had come down.

"And I've had so many compliments about my acting ability from the rest of the cast," Cat continued. "It's all been absolutely wonderful!"

She put her hand to her face and jokingly dabbed away an imaginary tear.

"But why didn't you *tell* us?" asked Kerry. "I mean, the lead role – wow!"

"I wanted to surprise you," Cat grinned triumphantly. "And it looks like I did."

"You sure did. And I've got to hand it to you, Cat, you were great," added Matt.

"My, a compliment from you, Matt Ryan. Will wonders never cease?" Cat purred. "Mind you, my surprise nearly backfired – I thought you lot were going to ruin it for me."

"What do you mean?" asked Sonja.

"Well, when I saw you'd practically taken up the whole front row, it put me off so much I nearly forgot my opening lines."

"You've got Joe to thank for that then. He queued for ages so we could get the best seats," Maya explained, as Joe shuffled uneasily in his Caterpillar boots, his face crimson.

"I... er... I said I'd be there in the front row cheering you on," he explained. "And I didn't want to let you down..."

What he was saying sounded pathetic now, Joe thought, and wished he'd stopped himself before he'd blurted it out.

"Oh, you *schweetie*," said Cat, planting a theatrical, red-smeared kiss on his cheek.

Joe felt like a reluctant five-year-old getting smothered in hugs by an overenthusiastic relative. Any vague flutters of romantic feeling he may have had for Cat disappeared in that one smoke-infused instant.

"Though in future I'd prefer it if you warned me," she wittered on once she'd let him go. "We actors are so sensitive, you know, the slightest little upset or surprise can ruin a performance!"

"What rubbish are you spouting there, girl?"

Cat's Fairy Godmother, in the shape of Vikki, had sidled up beside the crowd.

"Oh, everyone – this is Vikki!" Cat giggled, thrilled to introduce her new friend to her old ones.

"Hi!" Vikki smiled at them, giving them a wave of her wand at the same time. "Listen, Cat – I don't mean to drag you away, but we're all heading off to the party soon and the costume girls want to get us out of these dresses!"

Cat stuck out her bottom lip petulantly as she held out the beautiful skirts of her ballgown. "Aw..." she humphed.

"We'll love you and leave you then, Cat," said Ollie, leading the others away.

"Come and tell us all about it down the End tomorrow!" shouted Sonja.

"Thanks, guys!" Cat watched her friends trundle off and blew them a kiss as they disappeared down the corridor.

"Now, I've just got one thing to say to you," said Vikki, fixing her with a serious stare.

"What?" said Cat in surprise. Everyone had been so nice that she couldn't bear it if Vikki was going to say something to spoil it.

"What are you playing at, flirting with Prince Moron a minute ago? After him being so mean to you before?"

"Ah!" Cat grinned, now that she knew what Vikki was getting at. "I'm just exercising my talent as an actress!"

"How's that?" Vikki frowned.

"After all that flirting on stage, and after seeing how I well pulled it off as an actress, he's falling for me, isn't he? And I'm just playing him along. I figure I'll keep him dangling tonight at the party, and then as soon as he goes to kiss me – and I know he'll try – I'm going to—" Cat slapped her white-gloved hands together "—cut him dead! Preferably when everyone's listening!"

"Payback time!" shrieked Vikki.

"Too right!" said Cat, her eyes glinting wickedly and most definitely not innocently. "No one treats me like some sad little Cinderella!"

CHAPTER 18

• •

BACK DOWN TO EARTH

"Isn't it great to be able to have a lie-in on a Wednesday morning and know you're not going to get hassled by your mum to get out of bed before eight?" Sonja stretched lazily in her seat in the End, before settling back and taking another sip of coffee.

"Mmm," agreed Kerry. "And to know that you don't have to worry about what homework you've got to do for a couple of weeks? It's bliss..."

It was getting on for midday and the girls had managed to drag themselves out of their pits at home in order to make the short journey to the café for a caffeine pick-me-up.

They loved school holidays, especially the Christmas break which in a lot of ways was more exciting than the summer one. At least at this time of year, the foul weather was compensated for by the fact that you knew you were going to get loads of presents and have a great time.

"Have you sent off your uni applications then?" Sonja asked.

"Um, yes... yes, of course," said Kerry, tapping her spoon agitatedly against her coffee cup. "How about you?"

"Yep. The worst thing now is having to sit back and wait for them to reply. I just want to get on with it now. I want to know where I'll be living this time next year."

Outside the window, they could see Joe and Maya on the other side of the road, ready to cross. Matt and Gabrielle were strolling up from the direction of the station car park, where Matt had probably left his Golf.

"So I guess we're all at a loose end then," said Matt to explain the sudden influx of the crowd. "And it's only the first day of the holidays for you lot."

"Unlike you, for whom life is one *long* holiday," Sonja jeered. "One DJing job every week or two and you think that's hard work. I bet—"

Sonja broke off, her line of vision interrupted by the sight of someone outside.

"Uh-oh, look out, you guys," she chortled. "She's doing her Cameron Diaz look again."

The others looked out of the window and saw Cat strutting towards the café from across the road. She came steaming in, all clattering heels and rustling PVC, a pair of dark glasses perched on top of her head.

The last time they'd seen her was briefly the previous Sunday morning, when she'd still been high as a kite from her acting debut and its aftermath. She'd finally (and hurriedly) told her friends about how she'd landed the part, her struggle against the snobbery of the other actors, and her crowning moment when she'd told Glenn, her Prince Charming, to get lost at the cast party in no uncertain terms.

Then, quick as she'd breezed in, she was off again. Off to meet her new best buddy Vikki, to relive the highs and lows of the last few weeks over a large strawberry sundae in town.

On Sunday, she'd been bubbly to the point of boiling over. A few days on and she appeared to have regained her composure.

"Hi, guys," she simpered, lowering herself graciously on to the red vinyl seat next to Maya. Opening her bag, she casually pulled out a copy of the local paper and dropped it on the table.

"Didn't think the *Winstead Gazette* was quite your thing. Thought you preferred *OK* and *Hello!*" teased Sonja, knowing full well that there was a photo of Cat inside – in full Cinderella gown – handing over a cheque to the charity the panto had raised funds for. Sonja's dad had pointed it out to her already.

Cat fixed her cousin with an 'I'll-show-you!' stare and silently turned to the appropriate page.

Kerry gasped and pored over the piece, with Maya, Joe and Gabrielle craning their necks to see better.

Matt was pleased for her, but didn't let that stand in the way of making a dig.

"Wow, Cat – with that kind of media coverage, what are you doing slumming it here at the End?" he laughed. "Why aren't you having tea at the Ritz, with one of a long list of directors dying to sign you up to their next £50 million blockbuster? What's gone wrong?"

"Oh, very funny," Cat shrugged, "Actually, for *your* information, Matthew Ryan, there *was* a talent scout in to see the show on Saturday night."

"Really? Has he been in touch with you?" asked Maya, glancing up from the paper.

"No," Cat huffed, flopping her ams on to the table and dropping her head on to them in frustration.

All of a sudden she looked less like Cameron Diaz and more like Bart Simpson having a strop.

Sonja slapped her hand to her mouth and pretended to cough. It was the only way she could cover up the uncontrollable guffaws she felt rising from her stomach. She didn't dare look at anyone else for fear that she'd end up in complete spasms; instead, she stared at the table, studying a grain of sugar in an attempt to appear normal.

"So, you've definitely got the acting bug now then?" asked Gabrielle, full of awe at Cat's success.

"Oooh, yes," said Cat, lifting her head and picking up where she'd left off. "I mean, who cares about some stupid talent scout? There'll be plenty of others."

"That's the spirit, Cat," Maya praised her.

"Yeah, and even though I'm not really interested in all that theatre stuff you have to study, I'm seriously thinking of changing my course to drama after Christmas."

"Er, Cat – I know you don't want to hear this, but there are a couple of problems with your plan," Sonja found herself saying.

"Like what?" Cat replied defensively.

"Like you're nearly half-way through the first year of your course already – there'd be too much to catch up on. You'd have to wait and start next September," her cousin pointed out. "And another thing, your mum would go absolutely *spare* if you mucked about and changed courses, after you having to persuade her so hard that you wanted to do beauty therapy in the first place!"

"You're just trying to spoil everything, Sonja, as usual!" Cat snapped unreasonably, as she tried to hide her disappointment at hearing common sense. "Just you wait! You'll be eating your words in a few years time, when I'm living it up in Hollywood, starring in *Sunset Beach*..."

Joe smiled and realised how glad he was to have the old Cat back. It was a lot less confusing.

• • •

Ollie poked his head around the back entrance to the End-of-the-Line café at the end of his stint at the record shop next door and saw Anna still hard at it. She was loading the dishwasher (*For the umpteenth time today, I'll bet,* thought Ollie) and whistling something that sounded like *I Wish It Could Be Christmas Every Day*. Nick had gone all seasonal and stuck a copy of it – along with other old Christmas classics – in the End's jukebox.

"Hi, Anna," he announced and grinned as her head shot round in surprise. "How's it going?"

"Oh, hi, Ollie," she smiled. "It's been pretty mad; we had the usual Friday mum and toddler groups in, plus loads of people dropping in after they got back from Christmas shopping in the city."

"Christmas Eve... they're all leaving it a bit late, aren't they?"

Ollie had a broad grin on his face as he spoke, Anna noticed.

"Bet you only did yours this lunchtime!" she guessed.

"Too right!" he said. "Had my list... shot round the shops... no problem!"

"And how was the record shop today?"

"Manic, for some reason. Looks like loads of people are going to be getting second-hand CDs and LPs for Christmas. And I'm going to be more manic tonight – we've got a local firm having a do in the back room at the pub."

"Poor Ol," Anna said, giving him a sympathetic look. "So you're not coming out to play tonight?"

"Nah. You guys will just have to sample the delights of Enigma without me. You are going, aren't you?"

"Oh, yes – got to get into the Christmas spirit," smiled Anna, though the image of the long empty day stretching ahead tomorrow hung heavy on her.

"Good. Are you planning to get involved in this kissing competition Sonja and Cat are so keen on?"

"Somehow, I think I'll leave that to the experts," grinned Anna.

"Wise move. Listen, Anna," said Ollie, leaning on the dishwasher and looking earnestly into her eyes, as though he'd just read her thoughts. "I meant what I said about you coming to The Swan tomorrow too. Have you thought any more about it?"

Anna still felt uncomfortable at the idea of turning up in a busy pub on her own, which would be filled with happy groupings of friends and families celebrating Christmas Day together. Ollie was trying to be kind, but Anna had already resigned herself to twenty-four hours alone behind her own front door.

"Yeah, I might pop along," she said non-committally.

"Which means no," sighed Ollie, sensing her martyrish mood.

Anna smiled weakly at her friend, knowing he'd read her mind again...

CHAPTER 19

●●●●●●●●●●●●●●●●●●●●●●●●●●●

SNOG-ATHON

"I know you're going to tell me to shut up again, but I *wish* Ollie was coming..."

"Shut up, Kez," Sonja said brightly as she carefully dotted a couple of glitter stars on her friend's cheek. "And hold still or these'll end up on your nose."

Kerry stood in front of Sonja's bedroom mirror and gazed dolefully at her reflection. She and Maya had come round to Sonja's to get ready for the Christmas Eve party, but for Kerry, the excitement was dampened by the knowledge that her boyfriend would be stuck collecting glasses in his parents' pub instead of being in her arms.

"I know I'm being silly," Kerry said, "but it's our first Christmas together and I wanted tonight to be special..."

"As it is, you'll be the only sad old bag in the place at the end of the night who's not snogging anyone," grinned Sonja in an attempt to inject some lightness into the conversation. "Maya, on the other hand, will be after every guy in the place, won't you, Maya?"

She turned to the vaguely horrified Maya and gave her a wink.

"I *don't* think so," Maya replied, her nose wrinkled in disgust. "Getting off with lads in nightclubs is seedy at the best of times, but on Christmas Eve? Yuk! That has to be the tackiest thing ever."

"Oh, come on, don't be such a spoilsport," Sonja laughed. "*Someone's* got to give me a run for my money."

"You mean you're still on for this kissing competition?" Kerry asked, staring at Sonja in astonishment. "What about Owen?"

"Well, he's not here, is he?" said Sonja, shrugging her shoulders. "And it's not as if we're joined at the hip. I mean, I care about him – you all know I do – but it's not like I can even call myself his girlfriend, we see each other so rarely."

To Maya, it sounded like a show of total bravado. Sonja was obviously still stinging from the disappointment of finding out Owen wasn't coming for Christmas after all.

"Oh, yes, " said Sonja, smoothing her slinky top down and checking out her reflection in the mirror. "I've got this competition thing in the bag..."

• • •

When the girls got to Enigma at a time they thought was early enough, they had to queue for twenty minutes before they could get in – even with the passes Matt had wangled for them. When they did, the place was packed. And it wasn't even ten o'clock.

"God, it's cramped in here," Maya complained as they fought their way through hordes of revellers towards the dance floor.

"Yeah, but have you seen the lads?" Sonja shouted above the music. "Pretty good catch tonight. Should be able to find a few that won't be too much of a hardship to snog."

Maya looked around the darkened room: as far as she was concerned the place was dripping with dorks. She was surer still that Sonja was covering up her heartache with a lot of bluster.

Idly looking around the club in an attempt to spot even *one* guy she thought she might be interested in, Maya noticed Cat nearby with the two Dutch guys, Rudi and Marc. At the same time, Cat saw Maya and began frantically waving to her.

Maya sighed and made her way over, wondering if she was going to hear the same stuff about this stupid kissing competition from Sonja's cousin.

"Maya, you know Rudi and Marc, don't ya?" hollered Cat.

"Yes, of course," Maya frowned at Cat. "I helped you sell them tickets for the pantomime during one of The Loud's gigs, remember?"

"Yes, but these naughty boys didn't come, did you?" Cat teased them, waggling her finger at them.

"We're very sorry," the one Maya knew as Rudi began to explain. "My uncle, he took us on a trip last weekend – to see some big scenes."

"Sights," his friend corrected. "Big sights. Sorry, our English is still a little bad."

"That's OK," Maya reassured the boys, while trying to work out what a big sight was and if they'd enjoyed it. "Better than my Dutch anyway."

"Pardon?"

Uh-oh, Maya smiled to herself. *This is going to be fun. Not.*

"You would like to dance on me?" said Rudi.

"*With* me," Maya corrected. "You mean 'would you like to dance with me?'"

The boy looked delighted. "Yes, please! Thank you very much." He took hold of Maya's hand and led her on to the dance floor.

Instantly, Maya found herself in a tight clinch with a wet mouth firmly clamped on to hers.

"Woah!" Maya exclaimed, struggling away from his grasp, "What was that all about?!"

"What?" he asked, surprised. "You don't like to kiss me?"

"No!" said Maya, wondering how to put into words how inappropriate it was to do something like that; how she wasn't that kind of girl; how he was right out of order – and all in a way he could understand. Instead, she took the quickest route and did what Maya never liked to do – she lied.

"I've got a boyfriend," she shouted above the music.

"I'm so sorry – I should not have..." he apologised as he followed her off the dance floor.

Maya rolled her eyes to the ceiling and made a vow to kill Cat. Something told her the poor lad had been put up to it...

● ● ●

Sonja stood by the bar, listening to some smoothie try and impress her with his witty (or so he thought) lines of chat. Though she didn't let on, Sonja was bored. Her intention tonight had been to grab as many Christmas kisses as she could, to have a good time, flirt a bit, and forget – temporarily – about Owen.

But it wasn't quite working out like that.

"I'm just going to the loo," Sonja finally said, placing her orange juice on the bar and sidling away from Mr Smooth, who seemed surprised to see her tear herself away.

Sonja got to the Ladies and ran her wrists under one of the cold water taps. She studied her reflection and wondered what was the matter with her.

In the past, she might have thought that guy was vaguely cute – definitely worthy of a quick snog in aid of the kissing competition – and yet here she was taking refuge in the toilets.

Of course, deep down, she knew what was up. Every time he'd opened his mouth to tell her some story or other, she only found herself imagining Owen's lovely, honest, funny face looking back at her. Much as she'd tried, she couldn't get Anna's brother out of her head.

She had been upset at the mix up over his Christmas plans, and even though they had since talked and Sonja had realised how the mix-up had occurred, she was still a bit annoyed that he had chosen to spend Christmas with his mother rather than with her.

And who knows what he got up to last night? she fretted to herself, thinking of the work party he'd told her he was going to.

Deep down, she knew that Owen wouldn't run off with anyone else, but the distance between them, and the emotion surrounding this time of year, was playing games with her mind.

She put on her lipstick and decided to head back to the bar, snaffle a Christmas kiss quickly to get her score up, then go and find Cat to see how she was getting on with her head count.

When it came to the crunch though, Sonja couldn't go through with it.

She slipped back out of the toilets and made her way to the other side of the club, as far away from the bar as she could get.

• • •

Having lost sight of the others, Kerry, Joe and Maya found themselves standing by the edge of the dance floor watching the smoochers giving it loads in front of them. In true Christmas spirit the DJ had decided now was the time to slow things down and the dance area was packed with Christmas snoggers in the muted glow of golden and rose-tinted lighting.

Kerry looked on, her heart heavy with

disappointment. In the past, at times like this – and before Ollie came on the scene – she would have hidden in the toilets while the slowies were on. Now she and Ollie were an item though, Kerry loved to smooch with him. Pathetic as it might sound, it felt as if she was making up for all those years when she'd sat this part of the night out.

She carried on watching – spotting Cat with the Dutch boy, Marc, and Gabrielle inevitably in Matt's arms – feeling as miserable as she'd ever been on Christmas Eve.

Suddenly, she felt someone put their arms around her waist and kiss her lightly on her bare shoulder. Kerry spun round, horrified that a guy dared do that to her.

As she saw who it was, the look of fury on her face melted into one of complete adoration.

"Ollie!" she exclaimed, her smile lighting up her face and everything else within a two-mile radius.

"Hello, Kez," he replied. "Happy Christmas."

He kissed her again, only this time it was a proper, lingering kiss that left her catching her breath.

"I can't believe you're here," Kerry said when they'd finally broken away from each other. "I didn't think you'd make it."

"I wouldn't have missed seeing you tonight for

anything," Ollie smiled. "And it looks like I timed it just right. Do you want to dance?"

Kerry nodded. They made their way to the dance floor and wrapped themselves around each other, lost in the music and their love.

Joe looked on wistfully as Kerry and Ollie smooched. He wondered if he would ever find someone to fall in love with, someone who had as much love to give to him as he had them...

"What are you thinking about, Joe?" Maya asked, though she was pretty sure what the answer was by the expression on his face and the direction he was gazing in.

Joe turned round and managed a smile.

"I was just thinking... Do you want to dance?"

"I'd love to, Joe," Maya answered, giving his hand a squeeze.

• • •

Sonja was sitting on her own in the gloomiest part of the club. She'd been there for the last twenty minutes, gazing out at the throng of flirting people and thanking her lucky stars that she'd come to her senses. It was as if she'd been trying to 'get' at Owen, even though it wasn't his fault that he couldn't be with her.

In the course of the last five minutes she'd

been joined by Matt, who'd quickly waved the others over to the roomy table.

"So tell me again what happened to Gabrielle?" Sonja asked Matt, having only caught the tail end of what he was saying as Maya and Joe had shuffled in to join them.

"She had a row with her dad today over what time she could stay out until," he explained, "and instead of him letting me take her home at the end of the night, he gave her a twelve o'clock curfew."

"Oh, poor Matt, I bet you were gutted," sympathised Sonja.

"Yep, you could say that. I tell you, he was waiting outside the club in his car when I took her outside at five to. She wouldn't even speak to him when she got in the back seat."

"I bet you felt like going home yourself after that, didn't you?" Sonja asked.

"I did think about it. But then I thought, what the hell, it's Christmas Eve. And I could hear the beer monster calling me from the bar, so I came back in."

Grinning, he brandished the bottle he was holding and took another slurp.

"So how did the snogathon go?" Anna asked Sonja.

Sonja screwed her face up. "It didn't, or at least not where I'm concerned."

"What happened, did you lose your bottle?" Matt chuckled into his beer.

"No, it was just that I kept thinking about Owen and I couldn't go through with it," Sonja replied, looking at Anna pointedly.

Anna gave her a warm smile in return.

"So how did Cat get on?" Matt wondered, stretching his neck up and gazing around for their missing friend. "Don't suppose she found a Prince Charming in here tonight, but it looked to me like there were plenty of frogs about!"

"Oh, I know what went on with her!" Anna said, eyes wide. "I saw her on my way back from the toilets. She was helping Rudi get his friend Marc outside for some fresh air, 'cause he'd drunk too much. She said she was really annoyed because she'd decided Marc was pretty cute and she was just going to go after him, instead of bothering with the competition..."

"But let me guess – he got sick before she could snog him?" giggled Sonja, happy to have something to laugh about again.

"Or he got sick *because* she tried to snog him," Matt snorted, remembering Marc's pasty-white face when he'd glanced across the dance floor during the slowie and seen Cat in his arms.

"Oooh, don't remind me," grimaced Maya. "His mate Rudi pounced on me earlier and I'm sure Cat put him up to it – told the poor lad I fancied him or something."

"Hang on, though," Sonja said, pointing a finger at Maya. "If I didn't get a snog and *Cat* didn't get a snog—"

"I kissed Kerry!" Ollie interrupted.

"You two don't count, or Matt and Gabrielle. This is a singles only thing," Sonja corrected him. "No, it looks to me like the winner of the snogathon is... Maya Joshi!"

Maya looked horrified.

"I.. but... uh..." she spluttered.

"What? Weren't you kissing him then?" Sonja carried on, enjoying the fact that she was embarrassing the normally unflappable Maya.

"But *he* was trying to kiss *me*," Maya protested. "It was all one-sided!"

"Doesn't matter!" trumpeted Matt, laughing. "It happened, and in the face of no other competition whatsoever, in my book that makes you the winner!"

As the rest of the gang fell about in fits of laughter for the next ten minutes, the look of disgust on Maya's face said it all. She was *not* impressed.

CHAPTER 20

● ●

CHRISTMAS SPIRIT

Anna got up to change the channel yet again and still found nothing she wanted to watch among the kiddie films and endless Christmas episode sitcom reruns. She wished for the hundredth time that Nick had provided the flat with a TV that was modern enough to have a remote.

So it was Christmas Day, but so far, Anna had spent the morning much like any other day off from work. Got up, had a bath, washed her hair, put the TV on, made some toast, read a book, generally lounged around.

The only difference was that she had two presents to open, which had come through the post the day before. One was a £30 book voucher from Owen ("Buy one of those arty, New-Agey books you like so much!" he'd written on the card. "You know me – I'll just get the wrong one!"); the other was a gift basket of Body Shop smellies from her mother.

Nice, Anna thought, *but not very imaginative. It's what people buy each other when they don't know someone's tastes that well.*

She had to laugh – it was practically the same basket she'd sent to her mother, which spoke volumes about their relationship.

When she rang to thank them both, there was no one at home. Anna glanced at her watch – eleven o'clock – and guessed they might have gone to church: it's what they used to do when she was living at home. For some reason it made her feel slightly depressed.

Anna flopped back on to the sofa and toyed with the idea of putting a tape on, but in the mood she was in at the moment, she felt that every track she listened too might make her cry – even the loudest, happiest ones.

She leapt at the sound of the door buzzer, sending Pringles flying out of the tube that lay by her side.

"Emergency!" Ollie grinned, holding two crash helmets in his hands.

Anna gripped the doorknob and tried to work out what was happening.

"The pub's mobbed and we need more hands

on deck. It's an emergency. Can you help? Please?"

"I– I–" Anna spluttered for a second.

Ollie looked at her pleadingly, like some cute Andrex puppy.

She knew she didn't have a choice and she knew too that Ollie had set this up.

"Wait a second," she smiled. "I'll get my coat..."

• • •

"More Christmas pudding?" Ollie's mum asked Anna. "Come on – you deserve it, after helping out so much earlier!"

"No, honestly, I'm full," she thanked her, feeling stuffed full of food and totally spoiled. "I was just glad to help."

"And thank you not just for helping downstairs, but for keeping us from missing Natasha too much," Stuart Stanton smiled warmly at her.

She blushed at Ollie's dad's words, but felt it was time to leave. Anna'd had a brilliant time running around helping out – bumbling around cleaning glasses and even trying to learn to serve pints, which Ollie at only seventeen was still not legally allowed to do.

She more than appreciated their kind invite to

stay for Christmas dinner when the pub closed for the afternoon. But now Anna felt she should let the Stantons relax and enjoy some time to themselves.

"I'd better go – I've got to phone my family," she explained. "But let me help you clear up first..."

"No, that's *my* job!" said Ollie, whose paper hat was tilted over at a rakish angle. "But stay and put your feet up, why don't you? Phone your folks later."

Anna shook her head, then stretching over, she gave Ollie a little kiss on the cheek and straightened his paper hat for him.

• • •

The chilly air hit her as she walked back through the park towards home. Her face felt warm and glowing and she couldn't help but smile.

It's amazing how different I felt just a few hours ago, she realised, aware of how phenomenally her mood had changed. All thanks to Ollie.

She strolled merrily on, humming a few of the corny Christmas hits which had been blasting through the pub all afternoon. Then it began to snow, which made Anna laugh out loud, and soon she was running breathlessly through the park, arms outstretched, her tongue sticking out to try and catch the snowflakes gently falling around her.

She only stopped when she realised there was someone sitting on a park bench close by. In the beam of the old-fashioned lamp behind it, she suddenly saw it was Matt, sitting there all alone, oblivious to her presence, lost deep in thought.

Anna walked up and sat down next to him.

"Hi, Matt," she said hesitantly, unsure whether he'd appreciate the interruption.

He looked up.

"Oh, hi, Anna," he replied casually, "I didn't hear you coming."

"I'm surprised," she chuckled, "considering all the noise I was making. Happy Christmas by the way."

"Oh... yeah, of course. Happy Christmas," he replied. "I nearly forgot."

"So what brings you here on Christmas Day?" asked Anna.

"Dunno really. I fancied a walk after lunch and kind of ended up here, I guess."

"No parties at your place then?"

"Far from it," Matt scoffed. "Me and Dad shared a microwaved turkey dinner, then he left to go to some girlfriend's for the afternoon."

"And no Gabrielle?"

"Nah. She's doing the family thing. I wasn't invited. To be honest," he added, a note of sadness in his voice, "I don't think they approve of me. Still, I'll see her tomorrow – that's when we'll swap presents, sort of make another Christmas Day of it."

Anna felt an instant empathy with Matt. She also felt sorry for him and guilty that she hadn't been aware of his situation until now. She doubted anyone in the gang had thought to ask him what sort of Christmas he'd be having, least of all Anna who figured she'd be the only one spending it alone.

Matt was the sort of guy who always seemed to be doing things, who had loads of mates, a great social life, not the kind you would ever think could be lonely. But Anna could see it now, and she bet that sometimes he was almost as lonely as she was.

"So are you planning on sitting here in the snow for the rest of the evening?" Anna said lightly.

Matt chuckled. "Maybe not. I guess I'll go home, crack open a few beers and watch some telly." He shrugged and gave her a half smile that he probably thought looked engaging but which Anna thought was pitiful.

"Why don't you come back to mine?" she found herself suggesting. "I've got two crackers left over from the café. We could pull them, read rotten jokes out loud and then argue over which crappy film to watch."

"Sure, Anna, I'd like that." Matt looked at her intently, then gave her a broad grin.

Standing up, Anna held out her hand for him to take. They both giggled as she helped pull him to his feet and they set off through the snow-encrusted park.

It felt like the most natural thing in the world as they strolled hand in hand towards the park gate, two lonely souls slowly lost in a flurry of white flakes...

Sugar
SECRETS...
...& Resolutions

SNEAK PREVIEW!

"C'mere, gorgeous!" said a voice in his ear and his head was caught in an vice-like armlock. "Mmmmmmm-*wah*!"

Releasing her grip on Joe, Catrina Osgood ruffled his hair carelessly and disappeared into the crowds of party-goers in search of another face to suction.

Joe blushed furiously, glad of the muted lighting in the cavernous town hall. Cat might not have thought anything of her overenthusiastic slobber (just one of many she'd be dishing out), but it had suddenly reminded Joe of his recent bout of madness – when he'd thought for all of five minutes that he actually fancied Catrina...

But this New Year's Eve, it seemed that it wasn't only Joe who was feeling awkward as the party poppers erupted all around him, sending streamers flying into the air.

Wonder what's going on there? he asked himself, his eyes settling on a strange encounter between Matt and Anna.

Matt, with one arm still circled round his girlfriend Gabrielle Adjani's waist, had turned around with a grin on his face, obviously ready to bellow a Happy New Year at whoever was close by. At that same second, Anna – fresh from giving her brother Owen a hug – turned to do the same.

They were so close to each other, they could have kissed without taking a step nearer, but instead of reaching out instinctively and doing just that, Joe noticed that they both faltered, smiles slipping, before Anna moved forward stiffly and gave Matt a brief, self-conscious peck on the cheek.

Almost immediately, they swung their attention away from one another, casting desperate glances around for someone else to fix on. Or so it appeared to Joe, locked in his own little world of self-consciousness just a few feet away.

"Joe!" smiled Maya Joshi, bringing him back to earth. "I was just saying to the others that we should dip out and get some fresh air – it's too hot and mad in here!"

"Uh, OK," agreed Joe dubiously.

He certainly wasn't feeling at his most relaxed; his two kisses had left him pretty disconcerted (for different reasons) but he hadn't expected to be leaving the party quite so soon.

Maya spotted the confusion in his face and tried to spell things out a little more clearly.

"I don't mean we should go home, Joe. It's just that Matt says the door to the fire escape behind the DJ booth is open," she explained, motioning towards the black curtain behind the speakers and console where the music was blasting out. "We can sneak away for a bit – sit on the fire escape and, y'know, just hang out, all of us."

"Great idea," he grinned at her.

"Well, come on – help me round up the troops..." she grinned back, linking her arm into his.

• • •

"Anna says that if you look up at the sky just after midnight at New Year, it'll tell you what kind of year you're going to have," said Maya, tossing her shiny dark hair back and staring up into the deep, star-spangled indigo night above them.

"Pity she's not here to interpret it then, isn't it?" murmured Joe, squinting upwards.

"She'll be here – she was trying to track down Owen and Sonja, remember?"

Joe nodded wordlessly. The others had all promised faithfully that they'd follow Maya and Joe out on to the fire escape – as soon as they'd finished talking to people/gone to the loo/got another round of drinks in or (in Cat's case) had snogged any male between the ages of sixteen and twenty-three. (And there were a few hundred of those in the building for her to work her way around.)

"So what do *you* think the sky's trying to tell us?" Joe asked his friend, aware of her shivering slightly as she sat next to him on the open metal staircase.

"Well," answered Maya slowly, "I guess that with so many stars out, it means it's going to be a bright, exciting year. There are a couple of clouds over there though, see?"

"Uh-huh," Joe responded, following her finger.

"So I think that means there are a few hassles on the horizon, but since the wind's blowing them quickly across the sky, those troubles won't stick around for long."

"So clouds are bad, are they?"

"Not necessarily."

"What if we'd come out here and the whole sky was just a mass of clouds?"

"I'd say that it was going to be an interesting year, with lots of unexpected surprises hidden away."

"Maya, you're just making this up, aren't you?" Joe laughed.

"Totally," agreed Maya. "I haven't got a clue, really. Where is Anna when you need her?"

"Probably waiting for Owen and Sonja to come up for air long enough for her to drag them out here."

"Well, Joe, I guess we'd better start without

the others..." said Maya, changing the subject. Though what to, Joe wasn't sure.

"Start?" he asked warily.

"Resolutions. That's the typical question to ask, isn't it? " said Maya, looking at her friend with her dark brown almond eyes. "So what's yours?"

"Mine? I, uh..." Joe waffled, not sure what to say.

"OK, I'll go first. I would love for something amazing to happen with my photography this year."

"You did pretty well with it last year," said Joe of the year that was all of fifteen minutes in the past already. "You came second in that big competition, didn't you?"

Maya nodded, remembering with pride the shocking moment when she was called on to the podium to collect second prize at the art centre the previous summer.

"I know, but I'm not going to give up there!" she smiled. "Joining the photography club was one of the best things I've ever done – I just feel so positive about it. I know something really good's going to come out of it."

Joe was suddenly struck with inspiration.

"Driving!" he blurted out. "I want to learn how to drive this year."

"That would be cool," said Maya encouragingly. "Then we wouldn't have to rely on Matt for lifts everywhere!"

"Only one problem, of course," grinned Joe wryly.

"What?"

"I can't afford lessons and if I could, I wouldn't be able to afford even an old banger at the end of it."

Maya understood the situation. Money was fairly tight at home for Joe, since his parents had split up several years before. And filling in on the odd shift at the End-of-the-Line café didn't exactly bring in a whole lot of cash for him either.

"Another thing..." he continued.

Maya gazed at her friend, patiently waiting to hear what he had to say.

"...that's not even my real resolution."

"What is it then?" asked Maya, noting the nervous grin twitching at Joe's mouth.

"I, uh..." Joe turned to make sure they were still alone, before continuing quietly. "I kind of made this vow that I was going to give up holding out for Kerry..."

IS IT NEW YEAR, NEW YOU?

• •

Joe's top New Year's resolution is to get over Kerry, but it's not going to be easy and he knows it. In fact, he's already wavering – and it's only half-an-hour into January!

No doubt you've got loads of good advice for Joe – but what about your resolutions? Are *you* determined to change your habits once the clock hits midnight, or will you be bottling-out by breakfast? Take our test to measure the might of your willpower...

Look at the following questions and decide if your answer would be **YES**, **NO** or **SOMETIMES**.

I   What's in your head?

✪ Do you reckon that if you change your life, your luck might improve?

✪ Do you make up your mind, then unmake it just as quickly?

✪ Do you give up when things seem too complicated?

✪ Would you rather keep your dignity than risk goofing up and making a fool of yourself?

✪ Do you spend more time daydreaming than doing?

✪ Do you think people don't take you seriously?

✪ Would you like to be a lot more sure of yourself?

2 What's in your heart?

- ✪ Do you find it difficult to share your innermost thoughts with anyone – even your best mate?
- ✪ If someone came up and said they fancied you, would you immediately think that they were joking?
- ✪ Do you try to tune into your instincts when you're making your mind up, and then worry that you've not used enough common sense?
- ✪ Do you think that love isn't meant to be easy?
- ✪ Do you believe that other people are more lucky in love than you?
- ✪ Are you too shy to let someone know when you like them?
- ✪ Do you think you're destined to be unlucky in love unless you make some big change?

3 What's right with your life?

- ✪ Do you think that it's better to be realistic than overly-optimistic (ie it hurts less when things go wrong)?
- ✪ Are you happier to cut your losses than try for something you just can't have?
- ✪ Do you think it's better to think small and be happy when things go well, rather than think big and be disappointed when they don't?
- ✪ Do you like the idea of reinventing yourself?
- ✪ But does the thought of it scare you stupid?
- ✪ Do you think that making a New Year's resolution is a positive way of changing yourself?

4 What's wrong with your life?

- ✪ Are your confidence levels wobbly?
- ✪ Do you ever wish you had someone else's luck?
- ✪ Do you ever wish you had someone else's life?
- ✪ Are there more things in your life you'd like to change than there are things you're happy with?
- ✪ When it comes to tricky situations, do you dither about, rather than dive right in?
- ✪ Do you think that everyone except you is super-certain about what they're doing with their life?
- ✪ Would you like to wake up on January 1st and be someone else?

Count up how many times you answered **YES**, how many times you answered **NO** and how many times you anwered **SOMETIMES**, then turn the page to see what it means...

SO, IS IT NEW YEAR, NEW YOU?

• •

If you answered mostly **YES**

Change, as some boffin-type once said, is a very positive thing – but only if you're sure you want to do it! You seem a little wobbly round the edges when it comes to confidence and decision-making, so maybe launching yourself into a whole new you when the clock chimes twelve on New Year's Eve is a bit too much to ask. You're likely to end up making yourself promises you won't be able to keep, and then be totally disappointed in yourself. Yes, make changes, but try doing it nice and gently, and spread through the year. After all, what's the rush?

If you answered mostly **SOMETIMES**

The grass is always greener on the other side... so ye olde proverb goes – and as far as you're concerned, it's true! You think that if you could just change something about yourself, then everything would be wonderful. Luckily, when you're spouting your New Year's resolutions, you know these sort of expectations are pretty hard to live up to. Don't shy away from the idea of making changes (it's as good a time of year as any to ditch bad habits!); just don't be too hard on yourself if you fail. Remember – you've got the whole of the rest of the year to get things right!

Wow, Ms Fearless – you're happy to make big decisions all by yourself, with no one holding your hand or anything! You've got enough confidence to take a chance – but you're not too proud to shrug it off if it turns out wrong. So, go ahead and make those resolutions for the next year! If you succeed and it makes you happy, that's great! But if it all falls flat come two minutes past midnight, you'll feel good that at least you tried!

Sugar
SECRETS...
...& Revenge

LOVE!
Cat's in love with the oh-so-gorgeous
Matt and don't her friends know it.

HUMILIATION!
Then he's caught snogging Someone
Else at Ollie's party.

REVENGE!
Watch out Matt – Cat's claws are out...

Meet the whole crowd in the first ever
episode of Sugar Secrets.

*Some secrets are just too good to
keep to yourself!*

Collins
An Imprint of HarperCollinsPublishers
www.fireandwater.com

Sugar
SECRETS...
...& Rivals

FRIENDS!
Kerry can count on Sonja – they've been
best friends forever.

BETRAYAL!
Then Ollie's sister turns up and things
just aren't the same.

RIVALS!
How can Kerry possibly hope to
compete with the glamorous Natasha?

*Some secrets are just too good to
keep to yourself!*

Collins
An Imprint of HarperCollinsPublishers
www.fireandwater.com

Sugar

SECRETS...

...& Lies

CONFESSIONS!
Is Ollie in love? Yes? No? Definitely
maybe!

THE TRUTH!
Sonja is determined to find out who the
lucky girl can be.

LIES!
But someone's not being honest, which
might just break Kerry's heart...

*Some secrets are just too good to
keep to yourself!*

Collins
An Imprint of HarperCollinsPublishers
www.fireandwater.com

Sugar
SECRETS...
...& Freedom

FAMILIES!
They can drive you insane, and Maya's
at breaking point with hers.

GUILT!
There's tragedy in store – but is Joe
partly to blame?

FREEDOM!
The price is high, so who's going
to pay...?

*Some secrets are just too good to
keep to yourself!*

Collins
An Imprint of HarperCollinsPublishers
www.**fire**and**water**.com

Sugar
SECRETS...
...& Lust

DATE-DEPRIVATION!
Sonja laments the lack of fanciable
blokes around, then two come along
at once.

MYSTERY STRANGER!
One is seriously cute, but why is he
looking for Anna?

LUST!
Will Sonja choose Kyle or Owen
– or both?!

*Some secrets are just too good to
keep to yourself!*

Collins
An Imprint of HarperCollins*Publishers*
www.fireandwater.com